RAIN DOWN

Rain Down

A Crime Novella

Steve Anderson

INTEGRATED MEDIA
NEW YORK

ISBN: 978-1-5040-8505-2

This edition published in 2023 by Open Road Integrated Media, Inc.
180 Maiden Lane
New York, NY 10038
www.openroadmedia.com

RAIN DOWN

RAIN DOWN

THE FALL OF 2009

Oscar Alvarez is missing. Vanished. Without my friend Oscar, I got nothing. Oscar is the only one who believes in me. He believes in me more than I do myself. The fact that he's gone missing makes me worry. It eats away at me and it makes me start imagining, like I used to so much, what it would be like to climb up onto the Steel Bridge and never have to climb back down.

It's Friday. For the second day in a row, I look for Oscar on one of the four dingy concrete corners of SE Sixth and Ankeny, which is near Portland's actual center on a map, but far from its heart. This is where we always meet, where we go off to work together. By 7 most mornings, all four corners fill up with Latino day laborers—*jornaleros*, they call themselves. They hail anything that looks like a work vehicle; vans, pickups, old station wagons, even cargo bikes, this being Portland-town. It's already past 7:15 a.m. now. I pass through the crowd, the rare gringo here. I ask the *jornaleros* in my crappy Spanish, "*Donde Oscar? Tu ve' Oscar?*" No, they say, no one seen Oscar. And then they're asking me the same, looking me up and down.

"Of course I haven't seen him," I say—*that's why I'm asking all of you*. Even the old caballero who always knows something can only shrug at me.

"He'll be here," I say. "He always shows. If he don't, I'll find him."

I keep waiting and watching, though it's way past the pickup. Three days ago, Oscar and I were working a good job he had going for us. The job supervisor always sent someone over here in a pickup to get us. But no pickup came the day that Oscar vanished.

It's October and getting colder and I hop up and down to keep warm. I feel like that kid whose friend didn't show up at the school bus stop. I got no idea where to start looking. For all the time we worked together, Oscar never told me where he lived. He lived alone. I knew it was an apartment way out on East Powell. I guessed he wasn't too proud of it. I could relate. Where I'm living is a homeless hostel, one of many in the center of the city. Homeless Lifelines, the place is called. It's the first time I've had a constant roof over my head for a couple years, thanks to Oscar. To most people it might as well be a prison. Many of the men sleeping on cots in the open room around me have been in jail for this or that, most of it drugs, and some others in another kind of jail, for those guys "not right in the head." When I left this morning, the day receptionist smiled at me wearing my new work gloves as I passed through the lobby. She has a wide face and an even wider smile. I waved, smiled. Neither of us looking at that white board with the names and dates of boarders checking out soon, the one's whose time is up.

If I don't get more work soon, my name is going right to the top.

Now it's late morning, the weekend's coming, and the four corners have thinned out. The few jobs came and went. I got elbowed out a few times, and I can't blame the elbowers. Without

Oscar, these new heavy-duty work gloves I got on make me a big red flag. I'm just some sorry-ass gringo street dude in a shabby Oregon State Beavers starter jacket and stained work pants. The only thing missing is the cardboard bed and cart of cans and bottles.

Oscar knew how it was—as if he had also grown up in a Canby trailer park and not Guatemala, like he did. Oscar looked about twenty, but was thirty-two and seemed old-man-wise to me. I first met him last spring in Dad's Place on Grand Avenue, not a surprise there. There aren't too many bars left for guys like us; all the new East Bank bars and cafes might as well be West Side day-spas and downtown jewelry stores. We played Golden Tee, the golf video game. We had a couple beers in a booth. At first it seemed to me that Oscar had this power for excavating the truth. Day laborers weren't all Mexicans, he told me—they're Guatemalan, El Salvadoran, Honduran, even a few *gringos*. Oscar said we could help each other—I had the English while he had skills better than most subcontractors. He even gave me his old work gloves.

We got jobs. Some *jornaleros* trash-talked us in Spanish but I got the gist: just who did Oscar think he was bringing in a gringo when it was hard enough? Oscar told them: *it doesn't matter where we're from, we're stronger all working together, instead of divided like the powers that be want us.* Summer came and jobs kept coming for us. I wanted to quit a few, the way some supers and subs treated us, but Oscar told me to focus on the upshot. I had just enough pay to hit Goodwill for work clothes and the Laundromat. We hung out after work. Oscar had almost played pro soccer back in Guatemala, he told me. He was a forward, always wearing the number 9. A bad knee wrecked it all, though, and the knee hurt on some jobs, but he didn't complain about pain, not like I did. Not openly. When my back wanted to spasm and made me have to limp, he told me how to stretch it, take care of it, manage the pain.

People wonder what's wrong with me, what's my deal, why me. It's never like people guess it is. No, I don't have Tourette's or hear aliens (who make me scream at you); I don't pass out and piss myself in doorways and my face isn't fried brick red from all the sun, cold and wind, though my voice has gotten a little gravely. In movies and TV there's always something clear-cut that puts a guy on the street—war or disease, a priest or a cult, disability, abuse. Those'll do the trick. But homelessness can also just befall you. I first came into the city about fifteen years ago. It owned me ever since. Every job I had seemed to end up in Central Eastside—pulling auto parts, powder coating, dishwasher, heaving around furniture and pallets. Nothing lasted—if business was down, I was always first to go. I had the back spasms and limp, which did not help. Sleeping on the hard stuff made it worse, cardboard or not. As best I could, in the spring and summer at least, I'd try to leave the shelters and handouts to the worse off. I got by. I collected cans. I've had places to live and applied for plenty others, but the pavement always ended up kinder than the paperwork, than the questioning. I tried to look for work again and again, but things only got worse when the economy went to hell and now we're a year into it.

I know what people think. Suck it up, bro, and get a real job—you're only thirty-seven. But poverty's not that simple. The despair is worse. It's not just the dough you're lacking. In the same way the rich guy gets richer because he's pulling in the money and yanking hard on the strings, the chances for a guy like me sink faster than dead weight in the Willamette River.

I'm still on the corners, hoping for an after-lunch rush. I try to hail a U-Haul van but the few laborers left crowd me out. I take a look around. Any *jornaleros* worth a rip have gotten work already or given up. Only the users are left, passed out against walls as if lined up and shot where they shot up, mouths open, heads rolling around.

Oscar had started confronting these drug-taking types who were encroaching on the four corners and using us for cover. Most *jornaleros* stayed clear, let the druggies' have one corner of the four, but Oscar got in their faces, urging them to get help, stop making it worse on *jornaleros* by spooking businesses and bringing the cops around.

I stayed clear of that noise. Amy, my sort of ex, was a joneser herself. Oscar got out his power tool for that. He said I was not helping Amy by trying to clean her up the way I was. I was only prolonging her suffering, like you'd feed and massage a bull for the next bullfight. Amy is just a little thing with a delicate face and big eyes. She used to come find me when the tricks, drugs and rotgut got up on top of her. I'd get her cleaned up. Sometimes we'd move it to big bushes along the river, farther south past the OMSI museum was best, we could just stay in there the whole day. I could see Amy cleaned up for good. I told her it would happen. She is still young, her body strong despite the scabs and bruises and red veins in her eyes. But she started to go her own way more after I met Oscar. I still keep an eye on her, when I can find her.

It's afternoon now. I only have about fifty bucks left. I'd counted it out this morning on the edge of my cot, facing the wall so no one could see me counting it.

I rip my new gloves off my hands, and I exit the four corners and head out.

I have to change this up. I have to do what Oscar would do.

I unlock my beater BMX bike from its signpost, cross Grand and pedal through the old industrial riverside, under the Morrison Bridge on-ramp between the train tracks and river. The stretches of old cobblestone thump at my too-low tires and the bridge overpass hovers above me, its thick pillars monotonous square trunks not even good enough for chickenshit graffiti. The freight trains thunder past a block away, the barricade lights going ding-ding-ding. I pass the homeless village of tents, tarp and cardboard, carts and old bikes lining the way. Amy wouldn't be here because this group kicked her out.

I'm not looking for her right now anyway. I'm pedaling over to the job site where me and Oscar last worked. There's a chance Oscar is there. Maybe he was cutting me off? I have to be ready for that. Maybe I wasn't doing good enough work.

The job site is close-in between Morrison and Hawthorne. It will be a condo building one day. They had Oscar and me doing the demolition. The work's been rough. They gave me a ripping bar to tear apart rusty, grimy metal cabinets and built-ins and then they had us clear out the cellar, all kinds of ancient heavy equipment down there, pitted and jagged like boilers from some old ship. Oscar was so good the supers asked him for advice and let him use their tools, even a welding torch. Sometimes Oscar stayed later than me. He would make me go home, get some rest for my back and my dang nerves.

Now that I remember it: the last time I saw Oscar, he was going to stay after everyone else left.

At the moment the job is a skeleton of an old industrial building, some floors half exposed, the windows gaping squares, tangles of old metal and fittings. It's a job stuck in demo phase. A chain-link fence surrounds the site. A sign reads Tappen Urban Projex in big letters along with the words Green is Good. On a mockup photo of the condo building, boxes with windows protrude from a crazy-ass quilt of surfaces and textures, making the whole deal look like mismatched egg cartons stacked on their sides too high.

I stand across the street, watching. Inside the fence, various subs cover material stacks with tarp while others haul away tools, machines. It looks like a job on hold, if you ask me.

And no sign of Oscar.

I walk on over. Standing behind the closed gate is this big-shouldered construction guy, Manny, who I call Burly Man. Oscar didn't know the word but he didn't have to. Big Manny stands there looking like he has to visit the John but someone's using it. They got him standing here like a bouncer, which is weird. They never had a guard in the middle of the day like this, especially one that's not a tin badge. I talk to Manny through the chain link.

"I'm supposed to say the same thing to anybody that comes by," he tells me.

"What's that?"

"Sorry, dude. We're going to be down a while."

"Oh. Something happen?"

"Yeah, it's called the economy. That's my guess. Shit's so bad they can't even pay for real security."

"Thanks for not being a dick to me," I say.

That gets Manny smiling, but I meant it. "Listen," he says. "I used to be on the street. Take care of yourself."

"Thanks. Maybe something did happen though. Inside there, I mean."

"Now, I wondered about that too. But I ain't heard a thing."

"Okay. You know Oscar Alvarez, right? He got me on here."

"'Course."

"You seen him?"

Manny shakes his head. "We was all wondering where he went. I know I was. I figured you would know."

I don't answer that. Of course he'd think I would know. I shake my head, shrug.

"You got his number?" Manny says.

"No. I mean, I do, but . . ." Some guys on the street have phones, smartphones even. I could have had a cheapo one if I wanted.

Manny frowns and looks around and hands me his phone through the fence. I can't figure it out without getting aggravated so I hand it back, reading the number to him off my ragged little note pad. He dials, listens. I reach for the phone, give it here, but he only holds it up for me.

"It's in Spanish," he says.

We listen together. It's an automated message. It hangs up.

"You know any Spanish?" Manny says.

"Not that kind."

"Me neither, but sounds like one of those 'voice mail full' deals to me."

"Okay. Thanks again."

"Hey, we tried," he says, pocketing his phone, his eyes glazing over like he's done with me now.

"I don't want to keep you," I say to him. "But let me ask you something. You know of any cops coming around here?"

I have to ask about cops because recently I had seen two of them around the four corners talking to the *jornaleros*. Their names are Matt and Jack. They're not exactly undercover, but they're not showing off their cop balls either. In their Levi's and fleece jackets, Matt and Jack could have been any contractors wanting extra hands on the cheap. The truth was the duo wanted the word on the junkies and wannabe pimp dealers who slither into our little cut-rate labor sale using us for cover.

"Cops? Hell no," Manny says. "Not that I seen."

"That's all right. Thanks." I turn to leave.

Down at the corner, the developer himself is heading out a gate, name of Gerald Tappen. The guy has thick black hair, walks taller than he is, and wears an expensive parka and work pants that look ironed.

"Oscar knew that guy," I say to Manny.

Manny just nods.

At the corner, a nice-looking woman with dark hair and her chin raised stands next to a big shiny black Cadillac SUV crossover pickup, like a Hummer with more chrome. She goes around to the passenger side without a word to Gerald Tappen and both get in.

"Piece of ass there," Manny says. "That's Eva Tappen."

"When Tappen needed a thing done right? He always asked his supers for Oscar," I say.

"Subs didn't always like it either. But I seen he and Tappen arguing about stuff, too, how to do this or that. Oscar was always pointing out the hazards. The guy stood the hell up."

"Oscar always told him when a certain job wasn't right. Unjust."

"Unjust? That Oscar's word? Not bad for a visitor."

Actually, it was my word. More often than not, I was the one pushing Oscar to point out the pitfalls. Sometimes Oscar needed pushing in that department, despite what people saw.

We watch Tappen's SUV drive away. Then I leave Manny be. I don't want him to get in trouble. There were enough of us without work.

Amy has mud or who knows what on her cheeks like she smeared it on herself and snot running out a nostril nonstop like a bad tap. She came bounding around a corner and there we are, locking down the sidewalk on Grand. Blocking each other. Her tiny fingers can't stay put, her head stays down and her stare wants to drill right into the concrete at our feet. She has to be high. People go around us, talking into their smartphones. I step toward her, she lets me. I wipe at her nose with my sleeve. It doesn't make her smile like it sometimes does. She tries to go around me. I pull her over to the nearest wall and press a fiver into her little hands.

"Do not smoke this. Do not drink this. Don't even eat it. Head over to Central Women's Assistance—"

"They won't take me anymore," she says.

"Street Mama House?"

"Them too. Not even the Annex. And don't tell me Salvation Army or some other religious joint, they treat me like a fuckin' child."

"There's the Laundromat. Our one. Clean up in the restroom while your clothes are drying."

"Some'un'll just steal 'em."

"Do it anyway. Promise."

Amy nods. Her little face scrunches up. I hold her a moment.

"You still have the tent," I say. "Right?"

Amy nods again. She pushes off of me. "Hey, that new cafe off a Stark? They let me use the restroom. Be nice, they'll let ya."

We share a smile, and I let her go off down the sidewalk, and it's all I can do not to ask her when she's coming back. But I have my own trouble now.

I pass a couple cross streets and sit in a doorway, focusing on the other side of Grand through the jammed traffic. The police have a small storefront precinct across there on account of all the trouble. Sometimes I see Matt and Jack standing out front chatting with this or that cop.

Two quarters land at my feet with a clink. I start to say, "Hey, I'm not a . . ." but the wannabe do-gooder is already gone, texting with earphones on. I scoop up the change.

After about ten minutes I see Jack outside talking with a uniform cop. Jack is a woman, but she dresses like a man even when she's not pretending to look like a contractor. Right now she's wearing a Gore-Tex jacket and a Portland Timbers baseball cap, looking more like a dad going golfing. It's all smiles and banter over there.

"How's it going?" someone says next to me.

It's Matt, Jack's partner. His cap is U of O but the rest of him looks almost identical to her, only he's about a foot taller and Jack looks tougher.

"Hey," I say.

"Didn't mean to freak you out," Matt says, leaning on the doorway.

"All right."

"You been doing okay? Hanging in there?"

"Yeah."

Matt pats my shoulder, and begins to stroll off.

"Question for ya," I say.

Matt turns back, shows me a little smile. "Shoot."

"If I can't find someone, and I think they're missing, what's the best way to go about it?"

"Missing, like, you think something's happened to him? Or is it a her?"

"Him. Not sure. I can't find him."

"Does he have a phone?"

"Yeah, but, it's in Spanish. I mean, it's some message."

Matt frowns. "Makes things harder without a phone."

"I don't want one," I blurt, my voice raising. "All I mean is, it's just not like him not to show up."

"Well, tell you what: you can always head across the street there, check in with us. Tell them I sent you."

"All right."

"Or you can talk to me. Tell me."

"Okay."

"Look," Matt says, "I know you don't exactly trust us. But, we're not the old school. It's a new day, has been for a while now. If it's got to do with the four corners, we'd be the ones who might know something about it."

"I know. Still, I think I might know one or two places he could be yet."

"Fair enough."

And Matt strolls off faster, like he really wasn't leaving the first time.

It's getting to be late in the afternoon. I think about places I could go, but they are places I used to go, and I remind myself, again, that I can't just go to a place because I been there before. The only thing is finding Oscar. So I head back up Grand toward Burnside and the corners, hoping, telling myself that when I get back Oscar will show with some excuse he forgot to tell me about. Lots of *jornaleros* head back home to *la familia* for this or that emergency.

Among the traffic, I see Gerald Tappen's big black Cadillac SUV pickup.

I hustle along the sidewalk to follow but it's in the farthest lane on the other side. It stops at a light ahead. I run and dodge people but feel my limp.

"What the fuck? Freak!" a delivery guy yells at me. I keep going.

The light changes, the SUV rolls on. A break in traffic—I run out into Grand but more traffic's coming. A semi's brakes moan, horns honk, bicyclists yell. I'm in that video game *Frogger*. I zigzag, stopping and starting till I reach the other side. Two macho dudes in a parked mustang laugh at me so I lunge and scream at them and they roll up the window. I glance back over my shoulder to see Matt and Jack down the street, watching. I keep on going.

I lost the SUV. I turn down a side street, panting and sweating. And I see the SUV parked, two streets down. There's a coffee place there. I pull my jacket hood up over my head and come around the rear of the parked SUV, just as a man comes out the coffee pace holding a to-go cup. It's him—Tappen. He's talking to the air with one of those blue-flashing earphones on like some kind of cyborg robot. Vacation tan, white teeth, the Pearl District poster boy. He's changed into an adidas sweat top that probably cost more than my tent brand-new.

I walk up to him. He has gone quiet, listening to someone on the phone. He stares at me blankly. This Tappen has no idea who I am. And why would he? Day laborers just spontaneously appear from 7:00 a.m. and stay till whenever they're done for the day, as if formed right from this wet sidewalk. I step closer. That Eva women gazes out the passenger window, out beyond the street, unaware of me for sure. I pull my hood down.

"You still on the phone?" I mutter.

"We're working on that," Tappen says. "We are. I'm promising you, right here and now . . ." He's talking to someone.

That Eva women watches now through the SUV windows.

I stay there, my feet planted.

As Tappen listens to his phone, he stands stiff and looks pale as if he's just heard he has blood cancer. The guy has played sports, you can tell by the way his neck muscles stretch, but he also has something desperate about him, around the eyes. Stressed. Guys like this have their own types of pressure—credit cards, car loans and mortgages maxed out, taking on too many jobs to keep it all going, meaning his family never seeing him. The economy tanking did not help matters one iota. I should know. I know it all too well. Tappen seems all right. He has given us work and wasn't one of those scumbags who tried not to pay the cash at the end.

He hangs up. He seems to sense me, or at least he sees me in a reflection and he turns to me.

I say, "I'm not asking for money—"

Beep-beep-beep-beep—his phone rings. He studies me as he speaks into the phone, and something flashes in his eyes, and he squints at me as if trying to decipher some assembly manual. He holds up a finger like I should wait. "Hold on. I'll call you back," he says and hangs up.

He smiles. "You're that guy Oscar brought in," he says all loud, as if I might be retarded, or whatever the word for it is these days.

I nod, yep.

"Oscar said you could do whatever. Oscar was never wrong, I'll give him that. Right? No one's ever what you think."

"You seen him?" I say.

"Me? No."

"He work for you today?"

"No. Nope. A couple days ago he did—with you, right?"

I nod. "If you see him, can you tell him I been looking for him?" I tell Tappen my name, but he doesn't repeat it to remember.

"Sure, man. Sure," he only says.

"Okay. Thanks. Have a good one."

"No work just yet," Tappen blurts at me, kind of going out of his way. "Waiting for codes and shit. Fucking city," he goes on.

And I feel a little rush of heat run through me. Cussing for my "street" benefit has always rubbed me wrong. "Okay," I grunt.

"Oh, hey. You see Oscar, can you tell him we've been looking for him? He sort of left us hanging."

"I ain't seen him. That's why I'm asking you."

"I understand. Sure. Man, I just hope he was not doing drugs or something."

Always with the drugs—as if they're all addicts, all of Latin America, just junkies. Or did this Tappen really mean me, like I am the bad seed? As if Oscar would somehow be here if it wasn't for me?

"'Course he's not," I say, done with this. I start to go, yank my hood over my head.

"Okay. Later," Tappen says to my back.

I can feel him watching me, just like Manny and I were watching him. And it does not escape me that he'd said Oscar *was* instead of *is*. He said it twice.

I try an outside pay phone I know that's not broke and I get the same voice mail message in Spanish and I realize I don't even know if I got Oscar's current number. I never used it or needed it, he just wanted me to have it. I ram my hands deep in my pockets, all fists, my knuckles banging together. I pass *Oregonian* and *Willamette Week* paper boxes and want to kick them, knock them right into traffic. I haven't felt this way in a long time, and I'm glad Oscar isn't witnessing it.

I bound back across Grand, screw *Frogger*, screw the honks and shouts at me. Then I'm back on my bike and pumping the pedals as hard as I can, jumping curbs and swerving between people, cars, other bicyclists. I can't help it. The hot blood has gone to my head. I fly down a side street and a delivery truck almost hits me but I sneak by so fast the driver never would've seen me before I was dead.

I end up close to the river near the Burnside Bridge, past the skateboard park underneath, keep going north on Second till it stops. I leave my bike locked to a Dead End sign, my own little joke to myself. An elevated stretch of the I-5 freeway looms ahead. I head toward a gravel service road. A fence has a sign: No Trespassing. I know this railroad zone by the river bank like some know the house they grew up in. It's a waste-land of rail lines, overhanging overpasses, more fences. I'm still feeling out of control. I slap at my head. Kick at air. I need to get ahold of myself. I cross the tracks. I pass the remains of a homeless campout, keep going. I find the spot near the water's edge, looking out on the floating Eastside Esplanade with its happy bouncing joggers and bicyclers. Boats move along the river. Right above me is a low, leaden sky of that sooty concrete overpass and those squared pillars, so close the under-highway would hit my head if I was standing. At my feet are slimy boulders, gnarly wood flotsam, and mangy river crows with their frantic pecking beaks.

This is my spot. This is the place I go because I been here before. This is my good old hideaway, the only place that can stop my blood from boiling. No one else ever finds it. The boulders and logs help hide me. I'm cradled here, like I'm cupped in a giant hand. I look out. Across the river, the city skyline mixes with the West Hills beyond.

The best part, though, is my view to the north. Dominating the horizon is that black skeleton that is the Steel Bridge. I hold my knees to my chest staring at it and, in awe, I imagine the bridge collapsing and hurtling down into the dark mass of river. And I'm on that bridge when it goes. I think on that a while . . .

I hear sirens.

It perks me up, something about it. I stick my head out and look back toward the river bank no-man's land. I can see white forms and blue and white color; what look like the shapes of police cars. They're just beyond a boarded-up old railway switch house.

I make for the switch house, using bushes and the freeway pillars for cover. The shapes are definitely police cars, three of them—one unmarked. Police and rail workers mill around.

One cop leans against a fence, facing away from the scene while another holds him up.

A decrepit iron fire escape runs up the rear of the abandoned switch house, out of sight of the cops. I climb the thing, up to the top of the two stories. I'm sweating now, panting, pushing myself upward. I've always been curious but this is different, like someone's got a winch cable on me and they're pulling me up and in.

I get on the flat roof, crouching, and move across the splitting sticky tar. I approach the edge and look out, and down: The rail line runs through a shallow gully. The ties are oily and the earth dim. Along the tracks and ties, I see . . .

Blood. It's dark and drying, in splatters and pools.

Two legs lay beside the tracks, but they're not attached to anything. They're severed at the hip. Wearing work pants. One work boot, one foot bare.

One arm lays nearby. The hand wears a work glove, and it's orange just like my new one.

A torso, with one arm attached, all still clothed in a blue soccer jersey. The back of the jersey reads Alvarez and has the number 9.

Oscar was wearing it the last time I saw him. I'd bought the same gloves as his because they had worked so well for him.

I collapse. I slump. It's like someone dumped a truckload of sand on me. Then it's a hose of cold water. I tense up. I press myself to the roof's edge. My eyes search for Oscar's head or other arm but only tall grasses and litter line the tracks.

A police van pulls up below. Men unload investigations gear from trunks and cases.

My stomach rolls, pinches, and my throat swells up and squeezes. I turn away, feeling paler than the gray-white sky above me. I vomit onto the roof. I get it all out. My mind racing.

I hustle down the fire escape sweating, moaning. I jump to the ground too soon, wince at the pain in my ankles and shuffle around to the corner of this building that stands between me and what's left of Oscar. I cling to the wall.

I got to get out of here before they come over, before they see me. Farther away from the crime scene, from the way I came, I see a gap in the bushes. I scramble over like a crab and on through, to a hole in a fence. And I'm gone.

My eyes grow hot. Tears run down my face, mixing with the sweat.

Someone killed Oscar? I can't fathom this. Who would want to harm him? It just can't be.

I find my way back under the overpasses to my riverbank hideaway. The rain's pouring down now, and the freeway above mixes with it to create a thunder-like droning. It's dry here. I have a blanket stashed. I wrap it around me and stare at the grim Steel Bridge. I try to close my eyes. Tears find their way out anyway. I pull the blanket tighter; I stuff it with newspaper and rags to keep me warm. I'd given my sleeping bag to Amy. Another bad idea.

Again, I wonder what it would be like to climb that bridge and never have to climb back down. It's far from the first time I've had such thoughts. They reach back to before I came to the city and are probably what sent me here in the first place, fooling me into thinking I could escape them. It was way back in Oregon City, one foot out of Canby. I had it going on back then. That part of the Willamette Valley wasn't ever doing well, but I had a shiny king cab pickup, a brand-new model with every snazzy option, including multi-sport racks and canopy and a trailer for my new jet skis. The graphic airbrushed on the door read, Bruner & Son Construction. My dad had started his own business. I would have inherited it too, if life hadn't started getting up on top of me. The pressure. The demands. The fear of failing. I used to smoke back then, menthols. One day when lighting a Salem, I could feel my face turn into a stone mask. Then the mask shuddered, and it cracked, and it felt like the skin of my face had been ripped clean off. I felt like my heart hung out in the air, stinging, throbbing, dangling from a chain around my neck. I couldn't breathe. Tears ran down my face and my mouth wanted to scream but nothing could make its way out.

I was on a side street in downtown Oregon City. I couldn't move. I sat there in my truck, my cigarette butt embering on the dash, melting the new plastic. I tried talking to myself, I did. I had too much stuff—that was my whole problem, I told myself. So I was going to get rid of my stuff. Next thing I knew, I saw my glove box hanging open. CDs and cassettes, baggies of pills, pot and coke, and all my many credit cards lay across the seats and floor. My beeper. That bulky early cell phone I had then, that kept ringing all the fucking time.

My beeper was beeping away now, and my phone ringing. But I felt like if I picked them up I would explode; to me, they were grenades.

I had dumped out my wallet and the business cards and cash on the seat. I had such a great girlfriend then. I pulled out the photo of her and tossed that on the pile.

My cell phone kept ringing. The beeper. Live grenades.

This went on into the night. At dawn, I had managed to get all the truck doors open. Heaps of my stuff lay scattered on the truck and around it—wet suits, boom box, new clothes, electronics and more, some still in shopping bags.

I remember lighting another cigarette. My beeper beeped again. I should have just turned it and the phone off but I couldn't do that either. My dad was depending on me too much, but what if I couldn't make good? What if I failed? I remember thinking.

It was all too much.

I remember walking away from the pickup and tossing the keys over my shoulder at it. Tears ran down my face, I was shaking, and my chest felt like it wanted to explode.

I had walked down a connecting street near the old paper mill and made for the old Oregon City Bridge, narrow and tall over the Willamette River, the mist rising off the nearby falls. The bridge's arch was sheathed in concrete but its skeleton was all cold steel underneath, just like this one in Portland I can't ever stop looking at.

I didn't know what I was going to do, with myself and to myself.

Just like now.

In the morning, the sun gleams the city skyline, the metal and glass glaring. The sun can't find me here though. I have to know what happened to Oscar. I unwrap my blanket. I push myself up and I stand, aching as if suddenly ten years older. My back wants to spasm but I go easy.

I hit the sidewalks. Over at the mini mart at Burnside, I yank a newspaper from a recycling bin. I find the Metro section and take it to the side of the building, sit with my back to the brick wall. I flip the pages.

BODY OF MAN FOUND ON RIVER TRAIN TRACKS

Police are investigating a body found on the rail line running along the Willamette River near the Steel and Burnside bridges. The man has been identified as Oscar Alvarez, 32, of Portland and Guatemala.

No cause of death has been determined. A police spokesman said the body was hit by a freight train, which has hindered evidence gathering. No details were immediately available. The investigation is continuing.

I read it twice. A third time. I can't look up. My face aches, hot behind the eyeballs again. I put down the paper, between my legs. I sit there a while letting the bricks dig into my back, the wet sidewalk soaking through my jeans. It's raining out, then pouring. People pass, not even seeing me.

I don't know how long I sat there outside the mini mart, but it helps me focus. I need to think. Oscar would want me thinking. First, I find my feet. Then I pull off my telltale starter jacket, turn it inside out so it's dark blue instead of black-orange-white, put it back on. I go to the recycling bin, make sure no one's watching, and set the newspaper back inside. It's raining harder. The wind's picking up. I walk the battered sidewalks keeping one eye over my shoulder. I use store windows to check for anyone trailing me. I also see how dirty I am already back on the street, with a tangled beard growing.

Something catches my eye. There's a police car up ahead. It creeps along a cross street. I hug a wall and watch it pass.

I need to keep my thoughts straight. Still, my heart thumps hard and fast and I feel like I am falling, like I'd jumped off a bridge but can't hit water. Rants and raves collide in my brain. *This is what a guy gets for trying*, I think. *What a guy gets for helping. What you get in this goddamn world here where it's every man for himself.*

I near the Goodwill store wearing a stocking cap to help disguise me, holding my jacket crumpled in a ball. I toss it in the donations bin outside. And I'm already cold. I'll need another layer soon, but I don't go inside for one because too many know me in there.

On paper, I'm probably the only one who could have harmed Oscar. I will be their suspect. Of course I will. The thought of it makes my veins boil. I stomp onward and see a newspaper box and now I do take a running jump and kick at it. It knocks me back, on my ass. I bounce back up again. I'm pissed and steeled like I haven't been in a long time. A regular passer-by seeing me like this would have pegged me for a tweaker looking for a fight.

In a way, I am. I'm going to get to the bottom of this, somehow. If I can sleep under a highway, I can sure as hell do this.

At least the rain has stopped. I prowl the warehouse side streets and find the loading dock where I sometimes check on Amy. The tent is there and the flap's open but there's only a pile of trash inside, all to-go boxes and rags, tall cans and candy wrappings.

I make my way over to the four corners at Sixth and Ankeny. Most *jornaleros* are gone for the day. On the corner where the druggies hang, three guys pass around a forty. A radio blares out crappy FM rock. A shopping cart lies on its side, dumping out soiled clothes.

Amy runs with jonesers like these and I still can't take it, never could. These are her crew? Her lame-ass pimps? They're spilling half the forty, beer foam all over them. One crawls into the cart and they twirl him around, howling, hopping up and down. When Amy isn't tricking, she gives these rejects blowjobs behind dumpsters, in the same place they pissed. These bozos plunge their grubby hands down her pants.

Fists form in my pockets. But I put on a grin and march over.

"Hey. Hey. Turn that down a sec," I tell them.

The three just smile at me. I go and turn off their radio. "That cool?"

Two laugh. One glares. He goes by the stupid name of Deuce. He's always around. Of course he has a neck tattoo. One of his eyes likes to screw up when he looks at you.

"Guys, I need a coat," I say.

"They'll take the clothes right off your fuckin' back," Deuce says.

"That's right," I say. "Looks like you got some stuff in that cart there."

They laugh, a little too long. They're high for sure.

"Fuck it, brah. We'll give ya a coat," Deuce says.

"All right. How's about I take a look?"

No one answers, so I go through the pile and pull out a jacket with a padded liner and a fur-lined hood. It also has a ridiculous blingy dragon pattern. I can't help that. I put it on.

Two laugh at me with the jacket on. Deuce's eyes screws up tight.

"How much?" I say.

"How much you got?" Deuce says.

"It's your coat."

"Fifty bucks."

"Give you five."

"You got a joint?"

"Don't smoke."

"Sit down, dog. Sit down."

"That's okay. Listen, all you guys. I have a question: where's Oscar? Don't look at me like that. You know who Oscar is. He knew you."

They laugh.

"What did you do with him?" I say.

"What did *you* do with him?" Deuce shouts.

One of them comes around my side. He yanks at my hood, pulling me backward—

"You guys, leave him alone!"

It's Amy. She marches up wearing a jacket like mine, but the kiddie version. The three jonesers laugh at that.

"Are they fucking with you?" Amy says to me.

Deuce mimics her: "*They fucking with you, they fucking with you, baby?*"

I ignore them. Amy is swaying—she's high too. "Where you been anyway?" she starts to say to me, but two of them grab me. I swing at them and kick. We all tumble down the sidewalk. My shoulder blade slams at the pavement, my back cramps up and burns with spasms. I go black a moment, probably hit my head. All three hold me down, giggling, panting. Amy pulls at them, trying to pry them off me. Deuce pushes her away and she stumbles off. I move to get free and somehow I do because they're still too high to put up a good fight. I wince at the pain in my back, my shoulder.

"Emergency! Get him to a hospital," one shouts.

"Fuck him—got no insurance, dog," says the other one.

"I'm a doctor," Deuce says. He holds a paper bag to my face. A whiff of huffing chemicals bites at my nostrils. I turn my head away.

"We fix you up, *señorita*. That's what you are, right? Oscar's your *papacito*."

"No!" I shout.

"Calm it down, dog."

"Wait, no, I gotta puke," I groan, faking it. The three back off and I get free for good and scramble away, the three peering around for me but not seeing like they're in a windowless room with the lights off. I look for Amy, but she's gone.

I hobble away, favoring one shoulder. My goofy fur-hood jacket has a ripped sleeve.

I'll live.

I get back to the homeless hostel after sundown. No one mans the front counter, so I rush inside for the rest of my stuff and pass back out the lobby with my duffel.

"Don't forget lockup later," says a voice. The night receptionist at the counter, Mr. Doom-Gloom we call him, is gaunt with deep eye sockets like the innkeeper in a horror movie. I don't say anything. "You haven't paid," he adds. "Tomorrow's your last night."

I pause at the door hearing that, what he is really saying to me.

"And I will lock you out," he says.

"So lock me out," I say and push on out the front door.

The reality comes back to me, again and again. It makes me think about those detectives, Matt and Jack. They might be the only cops I could trust. They might even be looking out for me. I wasn't a betting man, never played Video Poker or Keno, having seen too many suckers fall down a whole so deep you can't hear them screaming. Still, betting on Matt and Jack was a wager I might have to make eventually. But they also could be playing me.

Then I realize that they're no different than anyone. They'll think I did it. Everyone will. They'll have to. They'll need to. I am expendable. No one really knows me, and the other half don't even know my name. Me doing it gives them some sense to their lives. A guy like me being made to pay is all they got to keep them warm at night, all those people who got no clue they are only a shot of bad luck away from being me. How far would a person like that go to keep that from happening? Would a person like that let a guy die?

It's only 8:00 pm, on a Saturday night. I'm wide awake. Things are becoming clearer. It's like Oscar himself has risen from the mire, reassembled, and passed to me his power tool of truth. It tells me, exactly, how it all could have gone down. But I need confirmation.

What do they always say in cop shows? Follow the money. Or in this case, the lack of it.

I head down Grand to Dad's Place. This building is one of the East Bank's oldest, and inside Dad's they got dusty sailing memorabilia on the timbered rafters and brick walls. It smells like fryer grease that needs changing and cigarette smoke blown out lungs soaked in cheap-ass well whisky. It can be old-school slacker like Portland used to be when you hit it just right. I'm not hitting it right. At this later hour, your so-called creative class youth fill out the place, mixing with the aging so-called trailer trash types, the blue-collar, lost souls, happy campers and the beaucoup sketchy, keno, video poker, vinyl booths the color of sewage. The waitress young enough to be a guy's daughter but looking like their New Wave girlfriend about 1982. Kids whose parents thought Portland was in Maine play lowbrow loser with their simulated raggedy-ass facial hair and factory-faded caps, but if they really knew what losing meant they'd run right out into the cold fall rain and keep on going, right for that sweet Iowa girl and the ad agency job they been denying too long. Dodge too long, kiddies, and you'll be living like me.

I'm down to twenty bucks, total. All I got left is this bone-dry truth Oscar gave me. I find Burly Manny at the far end of the bar, facing out, his pint emptied. I plop down next to him.

Burly Man gestures for a beer, to buy me one.

"I got money," I say.

"Save it," Manny says, "save it."

The beers come, two Ninkasis. Manny toasts me in the way a guy does when he's out of a job a while.

"Sucks about Oscar," he says. "Sorry, dude. Nobody gives a shit."

"I give a shit."

"You had nothing to do with it."

"You can speak at my hanging."

"Don't think like that," Manny says. "They round guys up? Talk to you?"

"No. They talk to you?"

"No. No reason to."

We sip our beers. IPA is too hoppy for me and I don't drink much anyway. It's just us back here up against a corner within the dim glow of video games no one's playing.

"Me and Oscar," I say. Fake another sip. "We talked about helping guys get work. Safe work. Don't matter who they are, we get 'em organized. Someday. Anyway, Oscar fired me up about it."

"He was good at that."

"Oscar liked to talk about it. But, here's the deal: I meant it." I was more into it than Oscar. Something always kept Oscar from committing, from helping me come up with a plan. He'd rather play Golden Tee or watch soccer games when we weren't working. But me, I'd had enough idling. "Quit dreaming, you know?"

"Sure. American Dream? Why you think they call it a dream—you're dreaming." Manny shakes his head. "Dude, you know how many guys that Tappen had to let go?"

"No, but this keeps up they'll have more *gringos* standing out there than *jornaleros*. Then who will all those immigration haters wanna kick out?"

"Martian labor? Fuck 'em."

"What about you? Still getting a check?" I ask Manny.

"For now. Tiny as hell. I do this and that, on-call. That condo job? Dead. They don't even bother with site security except for me on the cheap."

"That so?"

"Everyone's sweating. Blame the economy, they say. Well,

know what? Economy's not a person. So whose fault is it? Top dogs? Hell no, it's everyone but them. Same all over. Every douche out there thinks they were entitled to it all, they deserved it, and just because we're living in the US of A. Well, fuck it. Time to grow up, kiddies."

Two trendy young guys of the type everyone currently calls hipsters are making eyes at my stupid jacket. Burly Man goes quiet and stares them down until they look away.

"It doesn't bug me," I tell him. Those two are just as sheltered as I've been, in their own way.

"You're a better man than I."

I shrug. I take another sip, make everything seem natural. Me, I'm just sitting here. Stuff enters my head and I say it, no rhyme or reason. I shake my head at a thought. "I just can't believe that was the last time I saw him. Crazy."

"Yeah. Wednesday, right? I was right here at the bar already. You can tell the cops that."

"All the subs and supers had gone. Everyone. Me and Oscar were the last ones. I left Oscar there. He said he didn't need me. Said he wanted to finish alone. I wanted to help. He got pissed about it. He was like that sometimes." I shrug again. "He just wanted to be left alone."

"Okay so the guy did have his moods. Still. Someone had to come around eventually, make sure it was closed up."

"Like Gerald Tappen. Somebody like that."

Manny nods. "He goes by there every day, night, rain or shine."

"Even though the job is stopped?"

"Last I seen, he does. It's his baby. Maybe it's his last for all we know."

I sip my beer again. Somehow, it tastes better. And yet I want to smash this pint glass to shards, the way I'm feeling. Knowing that what I know has to be true. I'm almost shaking from anger, but I keep it inside. "I guess so," I say.

I have a plan. Before the night is through though, Amy will be needing me. So I head over to SE Oak near Eleventh and the old abandoned Bressie Electric building. All the veteran street people circle wagons here, safety in numbers. Their tarps and carts and worn tents surround me in the dark. I huddle in a doorway.

Amy comes to find me here. I figured she would. It's our little routine when she's had enough. She has the tent stuffed into a cart. She reeks of forties and cigarettes and whatever carcinogen was in that paper bag. We set up the tent, saying nothing, just like we used to as a team. We crawl inside, spread out our old sleeping bag.

"Take that coat off," I say.

"Who cares if we look alike? People are wearing garbage bags."

"It reeks. Put it outside to air out."

Amy lets the jacket fall off her shoulders and chucks it out the tent flap. "Now I'm chilly," she says, chattering her little teeth. I feel her nose—stone cold. I put my jacket around her. A tear rolls down her face. She probably can't even feel it.

"They didn't do anything to your friend Oscar," she says.

"Okay," I say.

"I asked 'em for real. I was with them most of the time anyways."

I want to spit, just thinking about them with her.

"They're not mad at you," she adds.

"Mad?" I laugh. I can only laugh. "They couldn't do Oscar if they tried, those jokers."

"I asked around, too. For you. I did it in Spanish. I speak good Spanish."

"I know."

She was an honors student in high school before she dropped out. She usually tells me that too. This time she doesn't bother. We huddle together a long time, just holding each other. The tent is only a two-man, but with her in here it seems bigger. She cries again, not out loud, just muffled shivers and sobs.

"I don't even want that stupid coat anymore," she says.

"I know. It's okay."

On my way back I'd bought her a little cinnamon roll and a banana from the mini mart so she'll have something special if she comes. I know she can smell it my pocket, but she doesn't bring it up. I hand her the food. She takes it, eyes lowered.

After she eats some, we sit there hugging our knees like two cold city kids in the woods who took too long to build a campfire. She whispers, "What if I looked outside and we were, like, at the Grand Canyon or somewhere?"

"Could be cold there too."

She looks to me, her eyes sparkling in the dim light. "Okay, Hawaii."

"Okay."

"I was there when I was a little girl. My dad took me there. Kona."

"I know. It must have been great," I say.

She turns away, facing the tent wall. I can tell by the way her shoulders shrunk that her little face has scrunched up.

"Look. I'm not mad at you," I say.

I hold her, rocking her. She snuggles up against me. I tell her:

"I want you to keep the tent. My stuff. I have a little money left. I want you to take some."

"Why? Where you going?"

"The ones around here will help you out. Just ask. I've

helped a lot of these guys. Don't look at me like that. Please? There's something I need to do. And the cops might come around meanwhile."

"What kind of cops?"

I think about mentioning Matt and Jack, that maybe they're different, but I swallow the words back down. "Any kind."

Amy pushes off me, sits up. "Why they always gotta screw with us? Only when it's a murder they can't solve, some rich girl ODs, just looking to vent or whatever, why not, here they come harassing us."

"This is not like that."

She stares at me as if I suddenly got three heads. "That's what they do though. You used to tell me that."

"I know, I know. But, this time? Don't fight them like you do. Tell them whatever they ask. Promise me."

It's only the tent, my duffel and about ten bucks, but it will help. I can tell she knows I mean it by the way she pokes at the tent fabric with her finger.

After a while, she snuggles up next to me again. We lie there. She coughs a little, but I tell myself it won't keep her awake after all that peaking out earlier.

"Thank you," she mutters, eyes closing, "for the food and stuff."

I wait till she's finally asleep, snoring now, a cute little rumble in her throat that won't be so cute one day if she keeps this up.

I wake in a sweat, a cold dribble under my clothes. That hot reality is back.

I pull the sleeping bag over Amy. I kiss her on the forehead. I bundle up, as quietly as can be. I leave the flashlight at Amy's hand in case she wakes up. And I crawl out the tent, zipping the flap tight behind me.

* * *

Sharp sawed-off rebar, barbed ironwork and gnarled bolts jut out everywhere. Demo scraps lay in piles, all jagged. This skeletal demolition of a building looks like a bridge on its side.

It's Sunday. No one's around the job site. The gate's locked up but I see no tin badges, which confirms what Manny told me. There's always a way in though—a guy just needs the right mindset. My mind is set. I eye the whole of the site, taking my time as I move around it. I find a way through the temporary chain-link. I tiptoe deeper inside, crouching low, on into the building. The recessed third story used to be a mezzanine level. I approach the ironwork supporting it. I study it. Test my footing on it. I begin to climb up, and up.

I hunker down up on the mezzanine. A heavy rain comes. Most windows are gutted so the wind and water blow right through, pinging at the exposed studs and girders, the drops flowing and trickling down along. I pull a tarp over me. I can see out, with full view of the street. The rain won't stop. It roars like gravel on this metal. Pools form on the scarred, uneven floors.

An hour passes, then two. A couple kid taggers sneak in, but I yell like the security guard and they clear out.

Part of me feels the urge I had all those years ago when I abandoned my new pickup and all my dad had built for himself, and for me, and walked out onto the Oregon City Bridge. That day was just as dark and wet. I had stood in the middle of the bridge's narrow two lanes, less than thirty feet wide across. I was alone. No traffic was coming through at that hour. The bridge had towered over me, rising up in a concrete-covered arch. I could imagine all the giant skeletal steel girders and spans and bolts just under that concrete skin. I knew how bridges worked. I had wanted to be an engineer but had backed out of it, intimidated by the schooling it took, and returned to working alongside my dad. It was the only way he had wanted me anyway.

I remember the rain had picked up. It trickled down the concrete, making it glisten. I stepped onto the walkway, and then onto the base of the arch, which had a nice, flat width to it, and I started to march right up the slope, and upward.

I felt mechanical, like this was meant to be. My breathing calmed. I quit shaking. When the grade got steeper and the wind harder, I remember I kicked off one work boot, then another for better grip, and I had kept climbing. I had needed to reach the crest of that arch, and it was all that I would ever need again . . .

I perk up under my tarp. A black SUV pickup has pulled up to the job site. It's Gerald Tappen. He comes in through a rear gate and wanders around, checking this, checking that. He talks on the phone flapping his arms and pointing things out, this is not right and that's screwed, hanging up and pulling tarp tighter over materials and electricals, surveying his mess of a job like a dog just thrown into a cage. Then he's standing right below me. His phone rings again. I move forward to listen.

"Hey there, good to hear from you," he says. "Oh, yeah, we're still at it gangbusters. Hear that? We work in the rain here . . ." There's a long pause while Tappen listens. His face loses color. "No, look. But, I—we—gave you our promise. I'm telling you, it's all on schedule. And you promised us too . . ." He looks around like he wants to kick something. "No. No. You do that? It's dead in the water. All of it. This thing will rot. Dead. We'll all have to start over. Please, listen . . ." But it's he who has to listen. When the call is done, the rain has stopped and Tappen sits, head in his hands.

I pull back but my foot dislodges a patch of cracked tile.

Tappen stands up. He shouts, "Who's there? You, up there! This is a job site."

The mezzanine is like a big balcony. Stretches of railing have been ripped out, leaving the floor exposed. I crawl forward, to the edge. I pull back the tarp and show myself.

Tappen straightens. His phone rings again. He delivers it to a pocket, keeping his eyes on me. "You want work?" he yells at me. "That what you wanted? Fine. Problem is, there isn't any."

I don't say a thing. I just stare at him. See what that does.

"I got more people coming any second," he adds.

The hell he does. His voice is harder, more deliberate, like a patrol cop telling me to clear off the sidewalk, that doorway's private property, you'll frighten the customers.

"Me and Oscar?" I say. "We were working right up here. And you know what? It's real dangerous up here."

"How'd you even get up there? I returned the power lift."

"We never had no power lift, not for us. We had to find our own way up. But you wouldn't know about that."

"Look. Come on down. We'll talk."

"Nope."

"Then, I'm coming up."

I nod. I stand up but stay where I am, grasping at what's left of a railing. I hear Tappen make his way upward, picking his steps so as not to slip. When he's made it finally, he looks like someone just slapped him hard across the face. He joins me at the railing. It's torn away on either side of us. It wobbles. He holds on with both hands. He looks out.

I point down, directly below to the first floor. There's a wide hole there, a gaping rift that shows a grisly dark cellar with spiky old machinery like the bowels of a steam ship.

"After I left that day?" I say. "You had to be here. You're always here."

Tappen looks away, out where this building was supposed to have real walls again someday. I let him look, take all the time he wants. He smiles eventually, but as if he's opening wide for a dentist. "Now look. Don't go getting all smart."

"That what I'm doing?"

Tappen's smile falls away, tumbles down. I can practically hear it splat.

I just shake my head at him again. I'm thinking, the police will never believe me. No one will. And why should they? No one knew me. No one sees me. I laugh at the thought, still shaking my head.

Tappen says, "Don't *you* go shaking your head at *me* . . ."

He lunges and grabs at my jacket, fisting big wads of it. I smell his warm stale breath, like fancy cheese and wine from the night before. I push off him and kick at him, across the knees. He stumbles and crouches, glaring at me, looking for a fast way out but it's too slick up here. I kick again and again, like I'm Oscar in the big game and Tappen's got the ball I got to get and Tappen claws at concrete and wet scraps of tile. Keep kicking like this I'm going to make the pros. I kick and lunge, hurling him to the edge till all I want to be kicking any more is air.

I got him pinned to the railing. The railing creaks and loosens.

Tappen swings and flails to grab my feet, break free, something. He claws at busted concrete, exposed bolts.

I keep kicking. The railing busts off.

The railing tumbles down. It bounces off the hole's edge with a clang and crashes into the cellar below. Clangs and knocks echo out a sharp, sick reverb.

Tappen's still with me, staring down. Something makes me pull back from him.

We sit slumped near the edge, panting, exhausted. The rain is back. It found its way through the beams above and it trickles down our faces, clothes. Like this, Tappen doesn't look much different from a guy like me.

"I didn't do it," he says.

"Who did then?" I say.

"I don't know. I really don't."

* * *

People don't usually invite me into their cars. Gerald Tappen insists we get inside his SUV, since the rain is hitting so hard we can't hear ourselves. I could live in this vehicle. The seats heat. All it needs is a toilet. But I don't tell him that. I glare at the big digital screen in the middle of the dash, at all the big knobs on my side alone. After that rain and sweat I'm not exactly smelling great, a little gamy even. Tappen reaches back and hands me a towel, white and soft.

"I can wash it. Don't worry about it," he says.

He doesn't even roll the windows down for air. Pretty friendly for a guy who almost got thrown off a ledge by yours truly—too friendly, I'm thinking. He drives me over the Burnside Bridge and I think we're heading for the Pearl District but he takes me to that little strip club in Chinatown, Magic Gardens. He smiles at me, like I should be excited. Yeah, sure, this is just what us homeless guys crave all day—I really, truly just hope someone will please, please take me to a strip club. Nothing against the place. It's like an alimony-ravaged boozer's man cave, with one rack for a dancer and a pool table almost touching it, the video poker always in eye's reach, carpet that still smells of the pre-smoking ban days. The skaters and kids in bands and eventually the bridge-and-tunnel flocks discovered it long ago, of course, so it has that going for it, but there's nothing doing at this early hour on a Sunday. The bouncer guy was camped out next to the ATM machine smiling at Tappen till he saw smelly me follow the man in. "It's okay, he's with me," Tappen says.

We sit in the only dark corner. I thought Tappen only picked this place so he doesn't have to be seen in his natural habitat with a guy like me, but I can tell he likes it here. He insists I eat something, please, please, like some sitcom maître d'. I go for the tater tots. I drink a Sprite, Tappen a Tanqueray and tonic. The songs the dancer picks sound like protopunk or later and they rock but I don't know the bands except for the Wipers. It's too loud to talk. Tappen has to huddle too close to hear me.

"I took you for more of a suburban gentleman's club kinda guy," I say.

"Yeah, maybe." A young dancer sashays over after her three songs, but Tappen waves her away with a smile. He shrugs. "Got to get your wallet emptied somewhere. They probably have a framed photo of me in back, says 'Sucker of the Month.' But they just keep my photo in it." He adds a laugh. "You know?"

"Sure. Sucker of the Year."

Tappen, nodding, throws back his T and T. He turns to face me. "You believe me. I saw it on your face. You stopped . . ."

"I didn't throw you down there too, you mean." I wipe at my face, rub at my temples, pushing around the heat behind my eyeballs. "I shouldn't even be around. The cops will find me eventually. Me and Oscar, we were always together."

"I could vouch for you."

"Oh, what—I was with you at the time? That it?"

"Sure, why not. I gave you a ride home, back to your, uh . . ."

"What? My what? Where do I live?" A guy like this, he's got no idea. Screw this. I get up to leave but turn back, grab the last of the tater tots, wrap them inside napkins and stuff that into my pocket. "Thanks for the tots," I say and stomp out.

He could vouch for me, or he could screw me good. They would always believe a guy like him, but never one like me. Who needs a world like that?

Tappen follows me as I cross through Chinatown heading for Old Town and the Steel Bridge. He flanks me and cuts me off, coming around a corner. Faces me.

"Here's the thing: I don't want trouble," he says, "don't need it right now."

"Me, I love it. It's just fucking swell."

"I'm only saying, you can be smart. You were smart. Doing what you almost did, it would've made it even easier for them to pin Oscar on you."

"The crazy homeless guy did it, you mean." I start walking again.

"Look at you. You almost act like you want it pinned on you."

I say nothing, keep going. They won't pin it on me where I'm going and either will he. Not right away they won't.

Tappen bounds after me, pulls me into a doorway. "The cops spoke to me. All right? They questioned me. I didn't pin it on you. I didn't pin it on anyone. Just said, I didn't know where he was and that was that."

What can I say now? I don't have a plan for this. It's almost like this guy gives a crap. Almost. I hold out my hands and keep them there like I'm hanging them out to dry. "I should've just split, hopped a train to Tacoma, goddamn Spokane, something," I mutter.

"But, you didn't," he says.

Tappen drives me back over the river. He insisted on it.

"Oscar had a Green Card," he says, eyes on the road.

Could that be true? Why didn't Oscar tell me? Why did he pretend otherwise?

Tappen eyes me. "That's right. He had one for a long time. Guessing you didn't know? Could've been naturalized by now if he ever had his shit together."

"He had his shit together. Don't give me that." I'm grasping at the door handle, about ready to bolt at the next stop.

"Don't get out. You're not hearing me."

"I am though. You know what I think?"

"What, what do you think?"

"You're a sucker," I say. "All this talk of we. Who's that—investors, rich daddy, what? All they have to do is just fund you, fund your addiction, this addiction we all have. Then you're stuck. It's too hard to get out. You have too much stuff."

He doesn't answer me. He only shakes his head.

He pulls up to the Rescue House, a Catholic homeless mission a few blocks from the Burnside Bridge. It's Latino night, I can tell from the line of poor and homeless lined up outside. We stop at the curb, slowly, keeping a distance. We can see just over the line's heads. Inside, Eva Tappen is serving food to people. She wears plain gray sweats and no makeup.

"Think they're gonna see a Maria," Tappen says but not like it's supposed to be a joke. We watch Eva. She has the long neck and big eyes of model types, dancers, actresses, her chest poised so perfectly there has to be something manufactured about it. A little lift, maybe.

Tappen snorts. "I thought it would make me legit, marrying a stunner like her. The real deal, you know? I mean, since we're bearing it all here."

"Are we? All right."

"It's an old story. Just have enough faith, and the rest'll follow."

"Hers seems to be working."

"What, her faith?" Tappen glares at me. "So, here's another thing you don't know—she's Oscar's sister."

He might as well have vomited in my face. My lips, eyes sting. I can't say anything, just glare back at him.

"How you think he—you—kept getting the work?"

"He . . . never told me."

"Of course he didn't. And you know why? Because everything's rigged in this world. Everything."

* * *

Someone's in my tent, I can tell. It only makes the aggravation I got going burn even more. It just better be Amy in there. For a moment I hope it's Matt and Jack instead, and the thought only burns me hotter. I hear coughs, muffled talking, cooing. I throw open the flap and burst in. Amy huddles in the near dark clutching a hammer in case it's not me. I can see she's hiding a brown paper sack between her and the tent wall.

"You came back," she says.

I sit as far from her as I can get, my back to the flap. She turns on the flashlight. It stands at an odd angle, illuminating us with grotesque rays.

"Whash the matter?" she says, slurring it a little.

I can only shake my head.

She moves closer, holding out a hand for me. I can't stop shaking my head. She moves to kiss me. I push her away.

"You're wasted. You smell like that coat. One thing I know? Amy—she's always wasted."

Amy backs up, frowning. I see the paper sack again.

"What all you got in there?" I say. "Huh? Rotgut, glue, lacquer?"

She glares at me, then holds up the sack. Something yelps inside.

I grab the sack and pull out a fuzzy puppy, its ears flopping. It licks at my wrist, and licks and licks.

"Isn't he cute? He's so cute. Isn't he cute? Look at him. God," she says.

I hand the puppy back to her. She hugs it and almost drops it.

"But, I got him for you."

"I told you I wasn't coming back."

"I thought maybe you would if I got him."

"It's a she. Where you steal it?"

"I got it for you."

I scoot closer, using the knuckles of my fists to move along. "Some deal, trick, what?"

She curls up with the puppy. She faces away from me. I can smell the booze and chemicals on her, in her.

"Where's this end?" I say. "Huh? Where?"

"I don't know. Why don't you tell me?"

I punch at the tent wall, rattling all. We face away from each other. I still feel a chill, thinking about what Tappen told me about his wife being Oscar's sister. After he laid that one on me, I bolted. Just shot out of his SUV without even mumbling a thanks. I could feel his eyes on me through his high-grade tinted windshield glass as I headed off into the shadows of the next corner. Now it's like I'm in shock, a guy just been in a car wreck. If Oscar kept secrets like those, what else was there? What else wasn't like he said it was?

"The truth? The way we're going? It's a ditch somewhere for the both of us," I tell Amy.

Half an hour later, we're still sitting there side by side, like two passengers on a bus that's taking too long. I'm waiting for Amy to come down a little, to lose the slurring.

"The cops, they never came around by the way," she says eventually.

"There you go. It's never like I think."

"So, what are you going to do?"

"I can't stay here. For your sake."

"Don't you mean for yours?" she says. "You're going to your hiding place."

I don't say anything. She knows me better than I do myself.

I thought I had figured it out. I thought Gerald Tappen did the deed. Now I'm back where I started.

I set out the tater tots—she loves tater tots—and a to-go box of Chinese food I found on the way back. "I came back to check on you. Eat up. Give it to your new puppy. It's up to you."

And I go for good.

I had made it way up high. I was standing atop the very crest of the arch of Oregon City Bridge. The dawn had given way to morning. I had a fine view of the river and surrounding country, of the misting falls and the old paper mill.

Faint blue-and-red flashes caught my eye. I looked over toward Main Street. Two police cars were parked near the side street where my abandoned truck sat. The cops inspected the scene, poking about and looking around . . .

I've always thought that I had waited too long to make my move back then. Now, as I huddle in my blanket gazing at the Steel Bridge just before dawn, waiting for full daylight within this cocoon of my own making, I wonder if the truth is that "back then" is only supposed to prepare me for now—for this bridge that I can't stop staring at. I really have nowhere else to go but climb that steelwork, all those crisscrossing beams. There are so many ways up. I had imagined them all so many times . . .

A flash. A flashlight beam catches my eye. It travels along ragged earth and rocks, nearing my hideaway. I got nowhere to go. If it's a railroad bull I'm screwed.

The light shines on me. Two silhouettes stand over me, but their arms aren't cocked like they're going to screw me. I squint at the white light.

"It's just us," says a voice.

It's Matt, the cop.

"Christ," I growl.

Matt and Jack somehow convince me to climb into their unmarked car parked over on Second Avenue. Maybe it has something to do with that I don't have a choice.

I have the whole back seat to myself. It's plastic but they got the heat on. They have a coffee for me too. It's a mocha. Only one person still alive knows I like a mocha.

"You found our tent," I say.

Matt nods. "Amy's smarter than you think, when she's not frying her brains out."

"It's not like her. Giving my spot away."

"Well, she's worried about you. Thought you might be getting bad thoughts."

Matt and Jack smile at each other like happy parents, then direct their eyes back to me. In the dim streetlit-dawn, the shadows show off the womanly curves of Jack's face. Her seeming attempts to resemble a baseball umpire don't always hold up.

"Mocha all right? Hot enough?" Matt adds.

I only shake my head. "If this was TV? You guys would be threatening to turn me over to the badass railroad bulls."

Jack and Matt stare, drawing blanks.

"You know, for trespassing? I'm living in a rail zone. Jesus."

"I thought the cops rough guys like you up for sport, make you stand in lineups?" Matt says.

"That wasn't no TV show. That was real."

"That was years ago," Jack says.

"So. And I was going to file complaints too—"

"We get it," Matt says. "No one listened. Well, we're listening now."

"Or? We just go and arrest you for murder," Jack adds.

Matt and Jack smile at that.

"Then why haven't you?" I say. "Instead you let me fucking dangle."

Matt shrugs. "We just want the truth here."

"Fully objective in our pursuit," Jack adds.

I try not to roll my eyes. "What about that guy Gerald Tappen?"

Matt looks to Jack.

"He's on ice," Jack says.

"Meaning what?"

"He has a nice place at the coast. Manzanita. Said he's heading there for a few days."

"That's not what's usually called 'on ice.'"

"No, it's not. We couldn't hold him."

I throw up my hands. "I asked you guys a simple question."

"What about him?" Jack says.

"Did you question him or didn't you?"

"We did."

"And?"

"Maybe we didn't believe him completely," Matt says.

"Hey, you quit drinking your fancy coffee," Jack says to me before I can follow up.

"I finished it." I couldn't help chugging it, it was so warm and rich.

Jack looks to Matt, her eyes wide. "Oh, you know what?" she says to him. "He's thinking that he got to us."

Meaning Tappen got to them, I guess.

They smile at that too.

"It doesn't work that way," Matt tells me. "Not so directly anyway. Not in this town. Be cool if it did—more like good TV, but it don't."

"Just what the hell are you guys talking about?"

"Gerald Tappen, who else? You're sitting there thinking that Tappen bought us off or something, had pressure put on us from powerful people." Matt shakes his head.

I shake my head back. "I'm not thinking anything. I swore off that a long time ago. And you know what? I think I'm tired. I'm going back to bed." I move to exit my back door even though they locked it from up front. "I appreciate the mocha . . ."

"Wait. Stay a sec," Matt says.

I have to roll my eyes now. "What, is this the bad cop part?"

"Man, come on," Jack says.

"Most cases?" Matt adds. "We find that people play bad cop to themselves."

Jack nods to that. "It's in their heads. All in here. Is it in your head?"

"I really, really do not know what you're talking about now. You're not going to arrest me?"

"No. Don't have a good reason to," Matt says.

I sigh. "Jesus. Maybe the old days were better. At least I knew the torture had an end."

"All right, fair enough," Matt says, and he and Jack share a knowing glance.

To which Jack says, "Let me ask you something—what do you think about a wire?"

"It's not actually a wire," Matt adds, "it's more like you're the wire yourself, and you tell us what you hear."

"I think that's called being an informant."

"Okay. Sure. We wanted to make it sound better."

It doesn't. "That means I'd be a witness. Right? You being the experts and all."

"Not necessarily," Matt says, and Jack adds, "Look. I know you wanted to figure this out yourself. D-I-Y. Street guys, you got good reasons for it. But in this case?"

"Ain't gonna happen," Matt says.

I sit there a moment, slumped down, the plastic of the seat digging into my hip. They don't seem to have anything on me, even they admit it. So some of the danger might be lifted. The problem is, I probably know less now than when I started looking for Oscar.

Then it hits me.

"Eva," I blurt. "Eva Tappen. She's the only one you haven't mentioned."

"You got it," Matt and Jack say at the same time, then chuckle at each other. "You are good."

I cough, clear my throat. I hock one out the window. A sweet coffee drink does that to me.

"She helped get Oscar here," Matt says.

"Eva did? From Guatemala?"

"Yep. And you know what else? She's his sister," Jack says.

I make my eyes go big. I sit up straight. "Is that right? Whoa. Who knew." I add another shake of my head.

"Crazy, right? She set him up here," Jack adds. "Gave him all kinds of chances. Oscar, he's had more chances than all those *jornaleros* out there put together."

"And you think there's something you don't know. That a guy like me could find out?" I snort at that. "You know what Oscar would say to this? Walk away, my friend. Stay free, amigo."

"The thing is though, you're not Oscar," Jack says.

"Tell you what. You think on it. But not too long," Matt says. "You know where to find us."

"Christ," I say. "You guys are too nice."

"So nice it could get a guy killed," Jack says in a movie gangster voice.

"What the hell is that supposed to mean?" Matt says to her.

"Nothing. Thought it sounded cool."

And I can only shake my head, throw up more hands, roll more eyes.

Matt and Jack didn't give me any more clues to go on than Gerald Tappen did, and I didn't want to hear too many because it would look like I was committing to them.

I don't go to Eva's home. I hit the Rescue House instead.

This way I can bolt if it gets weird, and if not maybe I'll catch her softhearted.

I stand across the street like I do. There's no line this time. Inside, I can see Latino homeless eating with their heads down as a man reads a bible to them standing.

Matt and Jack must suspect Eva Tappen of something, or they wouldn't be lowering their standards to test out the likes of me. As for Tappen, well, I just hope he's not looking to frame me in some way.

Eva comes out the door. I skip across the street, stroll up next to her.

She faces me. The neon cross of the mission illuminates our faces red like crabs on the boil. She doesn't have that look like people get, she's sorry but she doesn't have any change. She's taller than Oscar was. We're about eye to eye.

"I'm looking for your brother," I say.

Her eyes go dead a moment, just glass eyeballs on a wax museum figure. They fix on me.

"You should go inside," she says, with less of an accent than Oscar had. "They are still serving people."

"I'm not people."

"You're that friend he mentioned. He worked with you."

"That's right."

She lets out a deep breath. She glances back at the mission, and just walks off.

I stand there a moment, then follow. I keep after her. We head around a corner. It's darker here. I tense up inside, my ass tight. I usually don't follow people down streets like this.

She stops, pivots, faces me again.

"I was looking for him. Then I read the news," I say. "I'm sorry."

Her thick lips tighten and thin like she wants to hock one on me. "Don't be."

"I guess I don't understand."

She steps forward, into my face, her eyes above me now. "Go to the cops. Do whatever it is you're going to do."

"You don't think they'd believe me," I say. "A guy like me, that it?"

"Like you? Look at me. An immigrant, or whatever you want to call it."

She's throwing me off with this. My brain goes foggy, scrambled. I don't know what to say.

She says, "I really ought to slap you is what I should do."

She walks away again.

Then things unscramble in my brain like yarn strewn all over rolling back up tight in a ball. The blood pumps in my fists, thighs. "But what? You'll dirty up your pretty hand? Screw you, lady."

"Fuck you," she says over her shoulder, keeps walking.

I follow but keep my distance, because I seriously consider that she could pull a knife or something worse. I can't help giving her a once-over. Her skirt is shorter than her thighs long.

She turns and plants each foot like a bull rearing up, and it makes me halt, straighten up.

"You don't get it," she says. "And you never will."

Eva Tappen walked off for good. I let her. She knew the play and when you know the play, you don't go and give it away. I understood that. The play was the same, whether it was me outwitting a nut job in a dumpster alley, or some investment broker scamming the rich guy up high in the mansion. To get wherever you need to be you string people along, hinting at what they crave, feeding their fire.

People think those of us on the street make the dumbest

choices. Maybe they're not wrong. But that doesn't mean one of us still doesn't have the potential to be Einstein or Machiavelli or Buddha or all rolled into one. Matt and Jack might say I am capable, or good even. But Matt and Jack want me to be a certain way. I can't be. I am still doing this thing on my own. So I never reported back to them on my encounter with Eva. Those two will have to trust that I am copacetic, that I am a guy who might play along in the end. That's why I didn't say no, while not exactly committing either. Hopefully Matt and Jack don't suspect me. They want at Tappen. They want at Eva. Still, I can't help thinking there is something or someone else and probably untouchable. Eva could be right. Maybe I don't get it. Maybe it is right under my nose. Maybe there is some force I'm not seeing. A power.

Why not aim higher? That was what my dad always said.

So I decide to provoke that forceful power into making its next move. That morning, I make myself visible. Act like a guy on a mission. I show up at the job site where I'm still thinking Oscar bought it. The four corners too, of course. Even Dad's Place. I roam the Central Eastside warehouse streets. Pretend to use that working outside pay phone, let everybody see me. Try another phone I know. I do keep clear of the safe tents around the Bressie Electric building even though it means not seeing Amy—I just have to trust she'll hole up there. And of course I avoid my Steel Bridge hideout. Even the smallest animals need a lair.

I keep at it that afternoon, making a big show of it. I'm everywhere. It's food-score galore when you're out roaming that much, every trash can offering up something, people practically throwing money at you, when you couldn't give one fuck. I'm inviting the full force of it. I go fetch my BMX bike locked up down by the rail zone. I do the tour on two wheels. I show myself back on Grand, ride the whole damn traffic-clogged shit show of an avenue. I stop at corners to chat it up with sketchy dudes

I usually stomp right on past, not making eye contact. I slow down going by the police precinct. I wheel around, turn back. I stand in the doorway of the precinct with my chest out. Then I step inside, bike and all and linger as long as I can until the info desk cop asks me if I have a reason. This is balls-out of me, considering the Oscar incident, and I feel my chest tightening up. I mumble, "Sorry, never mind," and stumble out, rolling my bike along. My heart is pounding now.

That will make anyone watching think. Maybe I am a little paranoid, but, I swear I feel eyes on me. They might be inside cars, or vans, some luxury SUV. They might be watching from building windows, or atop buildings. Someone is watching me. A guy just knows. Coming around every corner I expect someone to come at me. All my instincts tell me to dodge those eyes on me, but I do not.

And yet, nothing gives. By late afternoon, I've had enough. For now. Tomorrow I'll start it all over again, a scene that could still get hairy unless my eyes were telling me lies all day.

I ride to the DEAD END sign down by the rail zone, stopping to look over my shoulder, making sure no one's watching, and I lock up my two wheels.

I settle in at my secret spot, staring at the Steel Bridge, its spans and girders thickening black from the dusk coming fast. I hear the drone-rush of I-5 overhead, the coming and going, speeding, slowing. The heavy hum lulls me. My eyes close . . .

My eyes pop open. It's dark out now. I think I hear rocks crunch, I straighten. Someone is coming, I can feel it, but I can't see them and I can't hear with the freeway.

My pulse thumps, throbbing in my fingertips, my sinuses swelling with fear. I stand, letting my blanket fall. I face the only way in. A sense of relief hits me, loosening my face like cool spray from a mister. Only Matt and Jack know this place, I tell myself.

"Not you two again," I say.

They say nothing. Where are they? I step into the darkness near the tracks.

"I thought I was supposed to go to you when I'm ready to play along—"

Hands clamp onto my upper arms from behind and hike me up. I jerk my arms free and bolt but I stumble over rocks and where can I go? Into the river? Hit by a train? I look back and see the black silhouettes coming, enlarging, looming. I fall, fuck. I get up, they kick at me, I go down again. They hold me there and roll me onto my side. I smell glue, no it's tape, hear it rip. "Wait—"

They slap duct tape across my mouth, wrap it around tight. I flail my arms, but they catch them and slam my wrists together. I feel the sting of a sharp edge, but it's no knife. It's plastic ties, zipping tight. Cuffs. They pull something over my head, a long stocking cap and tape it secure around my neck.

They hoist me up and carry me along, my toes banging at rocks and sticks, my head knocking against their shoulders. The fear blasts out my nostrils like I'm blowing my nose, but soon they're huffing and puffing too and slowing. They stop, panting. I make a walking gesture in place, like the most pathetic fucking harlequin ever seen. One of them pats me on the back and they let me walk alongside them.

We go the length of a football field, maybe more, probably out to the end of Second Avenue. They stand me up. I feel a shape before me, blocking the breeze. They open it and push me down on my haunches and shove me inside and shut it—I hear the clink of a lock.

I'm on some kind of bunk. I roll either way and only hit walls. I lift up and my head bangs the top, the stocking cap hood cushioning the hit.

"Help!" I shout, "Someone help!" but through the duct tape it's just a murmur and it steals the air from my nostrils.

No response. What I lay on is flat, firm yet soft. My fingertips feel the taut fabric.

I'm hemmed in on all sides. This is like a coffin. What if it is?

"Let me out!" I scream, but I might as well be screaming underwater.

I take deep breaths, calming my breathing till the fear becomes only tiny hammers tapping at my lungs. If this were a coffin, it's made for two. I feel around with head and hips and shoulders hoping for a window but only find rivets and framework and something taped over, probably the only glass I could have reached. Through my hood I sniff, smell wood and wax and a faint petroleum aroma like rubber or new plastic. I sputter a sick laugh under my tape and it sounds like a moan. And I lay there on my side, letting the tiny hammers ease altogether.

I hear a truck rumbling at idle despite the din of the highway. I think I smell exhaust.

Then I'm rolling, jolting. My eyeballs bulge in the dark. I bang my head again. The whole thing's moving. I press against a wall, hold on. My pulse races and the more I gasp, the less air I get, all made worse by this thick, black hood they got on me like some poor bastard in one of those CIA black sites.

If I could only talk. *Come on*, I'd tell them. *Let me out, we'll talk.*

We're moving faster now, out onto flat road. I'm being towed in my cage. Soon we're on highway; I can tell by the way the roadway echoes inside here. So I lower my head, and I enjoy the goddamn ride. I asked for this, after all.

The plastic handcuff bites into my wrist no matter how I let my hand hang or lie. It's attached to bars, what feels like a railing. It's night but I don't know how light it is inside here with this hood on. At least they've taken the duct tape off my mouth. The fabric around my lips is moist again from me breathing, then hyperventilating, and all that saliva and breath with nowhere to go is making me probably more sick than anything. I've been here about an hour. I shouted, at first. Banged that cuff again and again till my wrist bone stung raw. But no one's hearing me out here out in this dead-end suburb. Which this must be. It took us about forty minutes to get here, tops. Lots of smooth freeway, then what felt like boulevard, then the slow turning and smooth cruising of a suburb—a development, more like. They dragged me out and through a garage to get inside.

I put it all together, wasn't too hard. The smooth hum of that garage door told me it was newer. This is a house, probably a mini mansion of the type all those new developments had before the economy hit the fan. I'm going to go out on a limb and say it's a foreclosure on a street full of unfinished jobs and more foreclosures, probably people squatting in some of them. Who are not going to say a thing about a truck backing unknown cargo up to a nearby garage. This could be Vancouver or Hillsboro, but my smart guess is Happy Valley or West Linn, which is none too far from Oregon City Bridge where I just could not take it anymore. My dad and I used to work on new neighborhoods out here back in the early nineties, from Canby to Beavercreek, Sunnyside to Damascus. Oscar and I used to work some more recently. Hell, I might have even worked on this very house. Odors tell me a lot when they make it through this hood. I smell exposed drywall, Pergo glue, some dry rot maybe, so it might be a remodel. I can tell it was probably a squat at one point, from the festering food reek mixing with the moldy smells of a house left unventilated in a cold and damp climate like ours. A good whiff of the two together is worse than any guy on the street, like a sweat-drenched T-shirt left under a pile of decaying fruit.

I relate all this to myself because working things out in my head is the only thing that keeps me from freaking the hell out. I am screwed here. They can do anything they want with me and no one would know or care. Pretty much what I been asking for since day one, and I don't just mean today. So much for Einstein.

They were rough with me, all elbows and shoves, let me drop on the hard floor. From the echo clang of the bars attached to my cuffs I can tell there is no furniture in here. I heard them setting up gear at one point near me, and I just hope it's not something they are going to use on me.

My chest squeezes up again but worse, like cable is winding around it taut till there's no slack, and a heat blazes behind my eyes. "Shit, shit," I mutter, the drool coming out and not making it through my stocking cap hood. I gag. The fabric around my eyes turns hot, damp. At least the little warmth it brings is better than the previous tear stains going cold on me. I keep shuddering, because there's no heat on.

I try to close my eyes and then laugh at that move because, hell, I got a fucking hood on.

Doors open, close, muffled but nearer. Footsteps, two sets. I straighten up like I got rebar up my ass.

They bound into the room—one of them closer, the other pulling a door shut behind him. Flashes of mag light beam flash by my eyes under the hood.

My nostrils pump air with a sound like sandpaper grinding, can't help it.

"Calm the hell down," the one close says but low like he's trying to disguise his voice.

My hyperventilating sounds like a cross between a death rattle and a machine gun. I let it happen, to throw them off—

"Said calm the hell down!"

He smacks me across the cheek and temple, knocking my head against the railing. The back of my head stings hot from the blow, like someone bit right into my head. It would have been worse without the hood on.

"All right, all right," I mutter.

I let my breathing calm down. We keep still a while. He might be crouching but he's not close because I can't feel his air.

The blow helps me focus. Let's just get this over with. Maybe they can toss me off the Oregon City Bridge when they're done.

A white flash permeates my hood and stays on me. A spotlight.

The guy comes over and pulls off the hood. I breathe in that shitty air of squat foreclosure but it's ten times better than a drool and tears-soaked stocking cap. He holds the light between him and me, right in my eyes squinting.

"You killed him," I say.

The light flutters. He pulls back. He sets the spot back on its stand. The light is still directed into my eyes, and he crouches down behind it. It's dark otherwise. His silhouette is big. He wears dark clothes and has one of those stocking caps over his head with eye and mouth holes.

"No," he grunts, "no way."

The grunt makes me realize who it might be, and it makes me shake my head. I laugh even though it hurts my face. My realization, it practically fills me with joy. Joy just kicked Fear's ass.

The silhouette grunts again. I keep laughing, even though I might get smacked again.

"Keep it up," he says, "just you keep it up."

I let some silence creep in. He sighs to himself. I see his head shake even though this blinds me. More silence.

"Well, fuck me running," I say eventually.

Another sigh bursts from him like a shot of air hose.

He pulls himself up and he stomps out of the room.

Leaving that damn spot on. I squint my eyes shut, turn my head to the side. At least I'm getting a little heat from that lamp.

The big silhouette marches back in. The other one keeps his distance. He's got the stupid cap over his face too with the holes. They stare at me like two bank robbers who lost their way to the savings and loan and only I got the map.

My eyes look squinted shut but I'm really a kid pretending he's asleep, spying on his parent in the room.

"Tell us what you know," big guy says using his disguise voice.

"Someone used too much glue for the Pergo. I can smell it."

"What? You think this is funny?"

"Definitely not."

"Oscar. Tell us about Oscar."

"I wasn't the one who killed him," I say. "I know that much."

"Maybe you did . . ."

"What, that supposed to be a threat?" I raise my head, pop my eyes open letting the light blind me. "If it's a fall guy you want, get in line."

Silence. Big guy turns around. I see his hands raise, palms upturned as if to say, *What now?* The other guy just stares.

I sigh, like a balloon being squeezed out. "Why don't you turn a regular light on? At least turn this spot off."

Big guy swings back around to me. "No way."

"You forgot to change your voice this time," I say.

Big guy loses his voice.

"Go ahead," the other voice says.

Big guy gives another burst of air hose, then clicks off the spot. All goes dark.

"Happy?" he says.

My eyes adjust. A little moonlight comes in from another room, our room being some kind of den off the garage with one wall open to a living room.

I say over big guy, to his master farther back, "You should've just driven me to the next city, dropped me off. Done both of us a favor."

The man stands there frozen, a black silhouette on that wall like crappy street art.

We wait it out.

Me, I got all night.

"You weren't supposed to hit him," the man against the wall says to the big guy.

Gerald Tappen to Burly Manny, that is.

I tell them, "Just take your stupid masks off, will you?"

They do, slowly, like villains in a cartoon pull off rubber faces to reveal their true identities. Here they are, confirmed. Apparently Manzanita wasn't that nice.

"Happy?" Burly Man repeats.

"You already said that," I snarl.

I see Burly Man's teeth gritting, a white brick. "You sure are getting smart for a dude not seeming so smart."

"'Seeming' is the operative word," Tappen says, his voice thin, grave.

They take my cuffs off, get me a cheap fold-up chair and two for them, and we sit in a little circle in the dark like the lamest therapy group there ever was. I don't say anything the whole time. Tappen turns on a light in another room and some of its glow outlines us, not much, Tappen adding that they can't have too many lights on at once or it will attract attention. From who? I think. No one gives a crap about a street like this or even wants to know. A development gone bust is the rich successful family's severely disabled offspring sent away to some hush-hush hospice in the hills.

Then we're all staring at our feet. Like we're waiting for the counselor to ask who wants to go first.

"You weren't supposed to hit him," Tappen repeats to Manny, who lifts his palms again.

More silence. I'm starting to realize that maybe I am their counselor. That being the case, I'll let them hang a little longer here in their chicken shit-stained cage of their own making. It's the least I can do. Throats clear. Sighs. Nails are chewed.

"Why?" I say to Manny finally.

"A man has to work," he mutters.

I nod for him to go on.

"What did I tell you about the dream?" he says.

"What dream?"

"The American one."

We're just dreaming, I'm supposed to say. *Money talks, walks, and sucks you down like a cheap lollipop*. But I don't give him the satisfaction. I turn to Tappen.

"I had to treat you this way," he says, "after what you almost did to me. What am I going to do, invite you to a spa?"

"Do what you want to me. I don't give a rip. Don't you know that? Dumbshits. I got nothing you can take away. And sure as hell nothing you can give me."

Manny lowers his head. This is getting to be above his pay grade. I still don't think Tappen or Manny did it. I wonder if they're trying to solve Oscar's death themselves. Maybe Tappen's even hired an investigator. Meanwhile, I'm a guy in the way. Men like Tappen, but especially his masters, they want the truth revealed their way if ever at all.

"Do I have to do all this myself?" I say. "No? Yes? Okay then: this is the part where you tell me why."

"I wanted to see what you would do," Tappen says. "How you would react."

"Not that why," I say.

He throws up his hands. Keeps quiet.

"You don't know anything. Is that it? Not much more than you told me. But, there is something else. Meantime, you're not sure I won't go to the cops. So, now what? How long you think you can you keep me on ice?"

Tappen says nothing. He and Manny are having a floor-staring contest.

"I'm sorry," Manny blurts. "I'm sorry I hit you."

"You owe me a beer," I say.

"Whole keg," he grunts.

"Quiet," Tappen tells him, "Please." He leaves a space where he might have said, *I'm trying to think.* "You want something to eat?" he says to me.

"Not yet." I face Tappen, actually scoot my chair his way. He tries to keep his eyes on me but they keep lowering, shifting left. "I been doing some thinking about what happened to Oscar," I tell him, "And you giving me that joyride here confirms it. It had to have happened at that job site. Like I said from the get-go."

"*My* job site. Let's call it what it is," Tappen says, his voice straining to sound penitent now. I wouldn't be surprised if he goes and lies prostrate before me.

"Your work was what killed Oscar," I say.

"Whoa—what?" Tappen laughs, looking around like he's got his buddies with him. He doesn't include Manny.

"The real problem is the work," I say. "The way it's all under the table. That's how it's done. How everyone does it."

Tappen opens his mouth to speak. It hangs open. Manny isn't

touching this now. He stands, mutters, "I'll be out in the truck," and leaves the room, out through the door to the garage.

We watch him go like you would a drunk who has to go vomit. Watch the door shut behind him.

"What happened?" I say to Tappen.

Tappen takes a deep breath, sighs. "It was that hole. Like you said. Right down there below us where you almost threw me off. He fell through there, right into the cellar. It was late, everyone gone home."

"You were there. The only one. You saw him fall."

"No! I found him there. Already. What was I supposed to do?" His voice cracking.

What does Tappen want me to say? I feel sorry? I glare at him, squeezing at the frame of my chair seat. I don't feel my smacked face, got no back spasms now. The adrenalin's taking over.

"Keep going," I tell him.

"I, I tried to stop the bleeding. Oscar, he wouldn't let me take him in."

"Take him in? God forbid you'd call 911 to your precious job site."

Tappen shakes his head. "He was looking me in the eyes and he said to me, 'You have nothing.' Then he just . . . went. What the hell was I supposed to do, man?" He hugs himself, rocking back and forth. "I mean, what else could I do?"

Did he really expect a response? *Sure, you did just great—dumping him along the train tracks was a great call. You're a real self-starter. You deserve a bonus, no better, a kickback.*

Now I am the one with the spotlight on him. I say, "That newspaper report came from the cops said his 'body' was hit by the train, not that it killed him. They're gonna know something."

"He had no insurance," Tappen says.

"Me, I got no insurance. Lot of people don't and the ones that do barely—"

"You're not hearing me. We would've gotten a shitstorm."

"*We?*"

"Holding company. Developers. Investors. You don't know . . ." He lets the words trail off.

Of course I can't know. How could a guy like me? If Tappen only knew. I squeeze tighter, gritting my teeth, wanting to rip this flimsy chair apart right out from under me. "There is no 'we.' I got news for you. They use you—and you let them."

"What the hell are you talking about? You keep saying that."

"No one even has to give you orders. You just do it, do it for them, and that's the way they like it."

Tappen laughs. "Ah, I see. I'm the big loser here. Last thing you want to do is end up like me? Right. I'm the victim."

Victim was nowhere near the word I had for him. I just shake my head at him. "You know what? I think I will eat something."

Tappen sends out Manny for tacos. Getting rid of his hired meat for now seems to brighten his mood.

"You want that beer?" he says. "There's Coronas in the fridge."

"No."

"Who is 'you two'?" Tappen says.

"Huh?"

"When we found your spot, when we took you, you thought Manny and me were someone else. You said along the lines of 'You two, not this again . . .' Said you'd go find them when you're 'ready to play along.'"

I stare a moment. This confirms to me that Tappen and Manny probably have no idea that I've been talking to Matt and Jack. So Matt and Jack might well be on the level. Tappen probably thinks I have a homeless gang or something like it's *The Warriors*.

"Just a couple dudes I run with," I mutter.

"They anything to know about?"

"Only if you're hopping."

"I'm what?"

"Hopping a train. Riding the rails. One time they jumped off and found my spot. They just like fucking with me."

"Oh. All right. Forget it."

"You forget it. I'm sick of this shit. Tell me what you're going to tell me before Manny comes back."

Tappen nods, and stares at the floor a moment as if remembering lines.

I really want to kick him out of his chair at this point, but then I don't get a taco.

"You won't accept my money," he says, still nodding. "So, how about doing a job for me? As a transaction. Then it won't feel like charity. Sorry if it's not the best choice of words."

"Gee, Mister Tappen, when you put it like that and all wrapped up in a nice bow too—in the form of a fucking fore-closure squat of a dungeon, how can I refuse?"

"Just listen."

I really want to say, "How's about you take me to the nearest bus stop for downtown? And I won't tell the cops." But he might not like that answer. He might even add a bonus paycheck for Manny—or someone worse—to take care of me for good if he doesn't like it.

"I'm listening," I say instead. It's what a Machiavellian type would do. And so I listen.

I wonder if I should have taken the chance and told Tappen to go jump off a bridge like me, but it's too late now. He has given me the work. This day laborer is back.

When Manny returns his head is drooped and he's way past losing his mojo, like a guy who knows this is his last paycheck (*what are they going to do, fire him?*). Maybe he just ate too many tacos, some churros thrown in. He won't even look at me. But he brought me a bag of ice for my face along with my two steak tacos.

On the way out they let me ride in the back seat of the cab with them, but Tappen insists I put the stupid stocking cap hood back over my eyes, for formalities' sake—so I don't know what development this was supposed to be.

"I was thinking Happy Valley, but now I'm pretty certain we were out toward Oregon City," I say once we're back on the freeway and they let me take off my hood.

Neither speaks.

"Was it a boat?" I ask Tappen.

"What?"

"The little ride you gave me."

Tappen grunts. "Teardrop trailer."

"One of those tiny campers? Of course it was." I have to laugh. Probably cost him a fucking fortune too and this was the first time he'd used it.

"I didn't have a car with a trunk," Tappen adds as if it's an excuse.

"Should've just used one of your porta potties. At least I could have peed—oh, wait, I had my hands tied . . ."

"Sorry," Tappen says, after a half mile or so.

Manny drives; says nothing, never met us. Tappen's phone keeps chiming and buzzing and he eventually turns it off and sighs like a dusty cowboy sinking into a hot tub, but not in a good way.

I say to Manny, "About that dream again—why you think they call it a dream?"

He doesn't answer. Can't even shake his head. I see his worrying eyes in the rear view mirror. They're working on the road ahead like it's a potholed fire lane along a high ridge and a long way down.

"Can't blame help for doing their job," Tappen mumbles to no one in particular.

Back in Portland, they drop me off at the old abandoned Washington High School in the pitch dark. Manny tells me he's sorry again, then grunts at Tappen like a guy muttering thanks for a final crappy paycheck.

I remember the fast-moving swirls of pregnant clouds directly above me, shifting counter to the dark river running below. It began raining harder, running down the concrete in streams. The rain had stung my face.

So there I had stood, atop the arch of the Oregon City Bridge, in my bare feet.

I turned to the inside of the bridge, with my back to the river. Looking down, between the crisscrossing arch-work, I saw the police—and firemen—standing by below, squinting up at me. The bridge was blocked off. Locals were gathering over on sidewalks and roofs with binoculars, cameras and food to eat.

I remember thinking, if I came down, I would never be able to return to the life I had.

A voice from a megaphone called out:

"We're here to help you! Please, just stay where you are. We're here to help."

Rescue climbers were making their way up the arch, about halfway from reaching me.

I remember feeling a warmth swelling in my chest. I remember thinking, this was what normal people recognize as a feeling of liberation, of knowing they had found what they love in life. I remember smiling.

I had backed up, so that only the balls of my feet and my toes rested on the edge of this arch rising over the Willamette River.

Then I stepped backwards; I plunged into that abyss . . .

* * *

Gerald Tappen wants me to find out what Eva is going to do about whatever she knows. The problem is, he doesn't know all she knows. She won't talk to him anymore. He thinks I can get to her somehow, appeal to her. He never asked me to get rough. He knows me better than that by now. It's a pretty smart move on his part—keeps me on ice, in theory, and means he won't have to get rough. Like that smack on the face that I'm realizing now he might have paid Manny to give me, having seen too many cop shows, and then he pretended like he was shocked, just shocked.

Old Washington High is not far from my Bressie building tent. I head over. Amy is gone. The next morning, I'm feeling pretty rough physically—like I'd been sleeping on concrete, most people would say, but I already had that going for me.

I don't go look up Eva. I go find Matt and Jack before noon at Niki's, one of the few old diners left on the East Bank. It's where they usually do their cop break. I tell myself that coming to see them is not committing to a thing. Sometimes, committing gets defined by what you don't do.

Inside, retirees and social-service cases sit in old vinyl booths. Matt and Jack wait for me in a corner spot. I stopped by the Salvation Army on the way—I have on an old used Columbia rain jacket, a nappy stocking cap pulled down low and big dark sunglasses.

"Star sighting," Matt says. "Alert the paparazzi."

"Only thing worse than being caught by us?" Jack says to him. "Being seen with us."

So they will stop teasing I pull down my glasses like the battered wife in a soap opera, all we need is the ominous synthesizer.

"Whoa," both say. "Took one for the team, I hope," Jack adds. Whatever that means.

"I walked into a door."

Matt and Jack exchange glances.

"Just tell me what you want me to do," I say in my gravely voice.

Jack nods at Matt, who says, "Eva Tappen is at the Rescue House again this evening."

"Just don't tell me to play up the homeless bit or I'm walking."

"However you want to play it. Just approach her in a good light. Don't get maced or something stupid."

"I just want to know what happened to Oscar."

"Exactly. We'll be here the next three afternoons, from 2:00 p.m. till 3:00 p.m.," Jack says.

"Or, we could get you that phone," Matt says.

"No!" I bark at them. "Sorry. But, no. They're just trouble."

"Fair enough," Jack says. "Get freaked out? Come at a different time, leave us a note. The staff here knows us. Speaking of, they could get you some ice for that."

"No."

"Okay. Then, you good?" Matt says.

"No. Need a mocha to go. Quadruple."

I wait for Eva Tappen in a doorway across from the Rescue House. She must have seen me from inside, looking out those panes of glass. I've been here for two hours at least. Huddling in the half-dark, hands hanging off my knees. Staring. Her silver little BMW coupe is waiting for her parked under a streetlight. When she finally comes out she looks around, gets in the car, shuts the door. I stand and step out onto the sidewalk not five yards away. I keep staring but can't see in, the tinted windows reflecting the light. A full minute goes by. Maybe she's calling someone to beat the crap out of me, that or the cops.

The passenger door unlocks, and she pushes it open. I bow to the opening.

"How did you get that bruise?" she says.

"Looking for Oscar," I say.

"Get in."

I slide onto the leather seat, already warming. "I'd keep these windows down, I were you."

She doesn't. She drives us over the Burnside Bridge, past 21st and 23rd, heading for the West Hills, I'm guessing. She shifts a lot. She likes to shift.

"Why am I in your car?"

She shifts down for the next light. "Gerald is a silly man. Like all men." She looks at me, but not with the glare I expect. "You are homeless, yes?"

"Right now I am. I wasn't with Oscar."

She shakes her head at the thought. Right before the West Hills, she turns off and guns it up a narrow street that winds along the base of the ridge. A sleek new condo building looms, a garage door opens, and we race inside like we're in the Batmobile.

I don't want her to let me stay here. Despite her hard tone, she probably will. People have tried this before. People don't get it. Sometimes they have a certain kink, or they think it will make up for something missing in their lives. A vision flashes in my head of her cleaning me up, us making love. Won't happen. I'll ask to borrow a blanket or tarp for the road though. Meantime, maybe she'll tell me what really happened if I play her along.

"You can stay here, if you want," she says, like clockwork.

"I don't know. Maybe."

She laughs. "What am I, a realtor? You have to see the place first?"

The condo has an open layout with modern styling, high-end

appliances and fine wood surfaces—a simple and green-seeming design. Tappen probably built it; I don't ask. Eva and I sit at a dining table in front of the vast windows. The city skyline sparkles beyond, as if floating. She drinks a pink wine, but not like a drunk, swirling it with both hands like it's herbal tea. I drink a Jarritos, *tutifruti* flavor.

She says, "Gerald, he went to the coast. He said he did anyway. I don't know."

I stare out at the view. It's a long way down. The city lights tell me where things are, my constellations. I can see the river and the grim, dark Steel Bridge, its skeletal ironwork a void—the opposite of light. It always finds me, and I it.

"Look at me," she says, her face hardened up like bondo drying.

"Okay."

"Gerald met with you, right? In that shitty strip club, I bet."

"You don't know? Why don't you ask the man?"

"What did he tell you?"

"He said you helped out your brother. Didn't tell me why. Look. All I know is, Oscar was good to me. We talked about what we'd do together someday."

"Ah, yes. Someday. You will organize the laborers. Help the homeless. Lift yourselves up. Someday. Like you're two prisoners in a prison movie."

"It's not a movie. I was going to—"

"So do it. Quit your talking about it. You don't need him." Before I can reply she says, "Do you even know how many people Oscar was going to help over the years? He was always wanting to inspire someone, something."

"No. I guess I don't." She's right on cue, feeding me what I need, the true version I should know. My feet press at the floor, but these high-grade floorboards don't creak.

"You were only his latest project," she adds.

Project? My blood rushes to my head. I stand up. "Don't call me that."

"Shut up and listen." She throws back wine as if she'd just popped a pill with it. "Oscar, he . . . he needed help. If he had only wanted it."

"What kind of help?"

Her long arm shoots out and she grabs me hard by the wrist, her fingertips digging in.

"What kind?" I say.

She just glares at me, keeps digging in.

I push her off me.

She bolts up, knocking over her chair. She rushes off down the hallway.

I let her cool down a while. I stand her chair back up, and slide it close to the table.

Eventually I make my way down the hallway. Light comes from the bedroom. I smell a cigarette. Eva sits on the edge of the bed. She's smoking, rocking back and forth. Tears stream down her face.

I stand at the doorway. "I'm going to leave. Can I take a blanket?"

"I don't care. And I don't care how you smell. I smelled it all before and worse than this."

"I just want to know," I say.

Eva stands. Paces the room. She faces me. Her look says, get in here. I step inside the room. She steps within a foot of me and raises her chin, more like in defiance than pride.

"No," I say.

"You do not even know what I am to say."

"I'm not taking your money, or whatever you got to offer."

"It's what you do with it. This is what counts."

"No. Not even after a nice shower."

"How dare you."

"Really, lady?"

Her fists are showing, and I don't know where that cigarette went. In a flash I imagine it searing my eye.

We each step back a little, glaring around the room as if there are strangers here we really need to leave so we can have it out, right here and now.

"That job killed him," she says.

"Right. Go on," I say.

She paces in a circle. "Gerald, he killed him."

"What?"

"You killed him."

"Me? Stop."

"He looked up to you. You didn't even know it, you're so stupid."

"I said, stop. You're drunk or something."

She's still pacing, another circle. "No doctors for Oscar. No clinics. No help."

"What help?"

"Dreams, hopes, all this money. These systems we live in." Eva shakes her head and it shudders her body and she's swirling around and I lunge and grab at her upper arms to make her stop, focus. She sucks in air like she's going to spit.

"It was my idea," she says.

"What was?"

I shake her. She shows me teeth, slimy with the saliva of desperation.

"Gerald told you he found Oscar," she says. "He said he didn't know what to do."

"You wanted Tappen to leave Oscar on train tracks? Your own brother?"

"Of course not. That was his stupid idea."

"So he was just stupid about it."

"Yes."

I'm fucked, it hits me—maybe she lured me here to make it look like me, maybe Tappen was even in on it. What's she got? A gun, scissors, dropped something in my *tutifruti*? She wants to be free, but I won't let her. We struggle. She knees me in the crotch and the pain tears through me like I'm dunked in ice water, then it's boiling. I slump forward, bent over. She stumbles backward, falls against the bed and slumps to the floor, her back against the frame.

I lower myself to the floor, fighting the pain. Anyone witnessing this scene would have already suspected me of horrible things.

We catch our breath. She glares at me with a wild look on her face, her lips shrunk back over her teeth.

"I killed him," she says.

"I don't believe you," I say.

"He killed himself."

"What did you say?"

"He killed himself."

I leave. Just get the hell out. I don't take a blanket. I march off down the hill. The road down is steep, tree-lined, dark. I walk along the shoulder. There's a clearing. I stop there. Here I can look down at the city skyline. I get back in my sights the void that is the Steel Bridge—it's like a watch I need to keep checking. I'm not far from a steep edge. I'm not sure what I'm waiting for, or what I'm going to do.

Eva comes walking down the road, her arms folded across her chest. She stands next to me. We say nothing.

"He got me my first job," I say, after a while. "On the four corners. Oscar made them take me."

"He looked up to you."

"Hardly."

"You truly did not know that?"

I shake my head. "This one time? We were on a job, big subdivision out in the suburbs. Framing. Muddier than hell. The super needed Oscar, wanted me to find him. I'm looking and I'm looking." I have to shake my head again. "Well, I found him. Inside a honey bucket, of all things. He wasn't going to the bathroom. He was just sitting there. But his face, it was all different."

"Like he wants to cry, but no tears can come out."

"Yeah. Like those street guys I know who were in Iraq, Afghanistan. The thing is though? It wasn't the first time."

"He needed help. He couldn't accept that. To him he was either perfect, or . . . nothing. I tried, for so long."

Then it hits me, like a pigeon swooping down and crashing into my chest. I step back. I point at her. "You found him. You were the one. It wasn't Gerald at all."

She just stares at me. Lowers her arms.

"And then you called Gerald there."

She closes her eyes a moment. "Afterward, yes." It takes her a moment to go on. "Oscar, he was waiting for me there. He had called me. He wanted me there."

"To make you see it. See him jump. He wanted someone— to know."

"I tried to stop him."

"And, afterward?"

"When Gerald came, I begged him so. He must help me."

"You never told him."

"No."

"All he knows is, he has a mess to clean up."

We stand there a long time, looking out together. The wind picks up, and we let it smack our cheeks.

"In my culture," she says. "In my church, a man does not commit suicide."

"So, what—he would have gone to hell for it? That what you're saying? But the deed's already done, so who you trying to fool?"

She doesn't answer.

"Gerald was trying," she says eventually. "He truly does love me and this is something I'll probably never get."

"What's he going to do?"

"Where is he going to turn? Not to the cops. Oh, no. He owes his investors far too much. They would not like what they find out. These are not kind people."

"They're gonna find out," I say. "They all are."

"What makes you say that?" she says, straightening up.

"It's the way things work. We're all like these tiny, what do you call them? Marionettes. Ant marionettes. Even you. Gerald. There are forces pulling our strings, but we can't see them, get to them. We think we can. We can pull ourselves up on the strings, hoist ourselves up and up and it really makes us think we're getting somewhere. But it's only just a longer fall down."

A sad smile spreads across her face. "You might be smarter than you look."

"Or smell?" I joke, but my smile won't hold. "I don't know. The jury's still out. Gerald's the accomplice. But I'm still liable."

I don't wait for her to answer that. I turn and descend the dark road, the steep grade propelling me downward, ever faster.

I don't remember hitting the water. I remember the dim vast river hurtling at me. A moment of nothing. I remember the shock of cold water submerging me. I should have never come back up from underwater. No one had survived a jump off the Oregon City Bridge. But I fought the water. Paddled. Got free. I burst up from below. I remember screaming and gasping for air as the river carried me along. I treaded water, though it didn't seem to work right. The pains in my back were so bad, I thought river rocks were pounding at me.

The shore came up fast, wanting to pass me. I paddled my way for it.

If I could have seen myself as I am now back then, I might have just opened my mouth wide and let myself sink down forever. Because I now have a beard, it's going matted and crusty, and I'm draped in a creepy overcoat and a thin rain poncho.

I had to abandon my hideaway to avoid Matt and Jack. I stay on the move. Tappen can't find me either. He'd given me a number to call when he let me loose with a long leash. But I still don't have a phone.

I keep telling myself: there must be some reason why a guy like Oscar does himself in and why I don't get to. Why should I survive? It's like his message to me.

It's two weeks later. I've been looking for Amy ever since I left Eva Tappen that night. No one has seen Amy. It's raining, almost snow. It's late afternoon but dim as dusk. I roam the Central Eastside, eyeing more dumpsters and places to take cover. I pass the day laborer corners and don't want to look, but I have to. Many more men crowd the corners but no one's stopping to pick them up. There's a growing group of *gringos*. More woman are there. All are looking for work now.

Burly Man eyes me from a corner, the only one seeing me. I nod. He's not working for Gerald Tappen now, apparently. I was his last day.

I wonder, again, what Tappen's game was. I wasn't just his informant. Maybe he wasn't going to frame me some way— maybe he was only trying to force Eva's hand. Well, I'm not going to let myself be his power tool, not anyone's.

I push onward. I've been to the loading docks multiple times a day but I have to try it again, like I have Tourette's for it.

Under the Morrison Bridge a guy comes flying around the corner looking for me. It's Amy's buddy, Deuce, the screw-eyed joneser who adores sharing his paper bag.

"Where is she?" I shout.

"Come on," Deuce says, his voice wanting to break in two.

He leads me to a fenced-in junkyard block of car carcasses, engines, scrap metal and oily puddle-choked gravel. Deuce has a hole in the fence. Inside, my tent stands in a far corner.

I rip open the tent flap as Deuce stands back. "Ah, fuckin' reeks man," he says.

I fumble for the flashlight, click it on. Amy lies on her back, her face pale. Vomit is everywhere. Syringes and huffing chemicals lie around. I should impale Deuce on something sharp but there's no time.

I take their grocery cart, haul Amy into it and, panting and limping, push the thing along and out and of course it has a bad wheel that rattles. Down the street, I see a pay phone but no receiver.

A car rolls up and I wave at it. It speeds away and who can blame it? I feel Amy's pulse. I kiss her on the head. Another car comes. I heave the cart out to block the street and wave my arms shouting, "Stop! Help! Stop, you!"

The car honks, keeps going. I push the cart onward, my lungs burning, right down the middle of the street. Headlights find us, light us up.

A cab stops. The driver jumps out. He's black and has an accent. "Get her in, mon," he says.

"I got no money."

"I don either, my brother."

We drop her off at Emergency. I don't go inside. I take a long look back at all the lights and warmth inside the hospital and I shuffle away, suddenly exhausted.

The next morning at dawn, I'm sitting in a doorway next to train tracks up north of the Broadway Bridge. I have all my stuff, one duffel bag full. This is it. Freight trains stop here a lot. The next one that does, I find a car with an open door and I hop and I go. I only hope it goes somewhere warm, because I'm shaking.

I keep telling myself: I can and I will start over, and I don't need Oscar now. I don't need any of them.

An unmarked police car pulls up. I look around for a way out, but it's too late to run and I'm too damn tired. The car stops. Matt is driving. The passenger front window rolls down—it's Jack. "We gave you twenty bucks," she says.

"Yeah, well, you want a guy to get a job done . . ."

"Don't give him the money upfront—I know, I know."

"Get in," Matt says.

I climb in back. Someone else is there. It's Gerald Tappen. He's slumped down wearing sunglasses and has Jack's Timbers hat on pulled down low. He has a scraggly beard, a cheap raincoat. Hell, like this, we could almost be twins.

"Lookee who we found," Jack says grinning like it's Amy's puppy.

Then I see the gauze bandage covering the other side of Tappen's face, and the way he's sitting stiffly like maybe he took some in the ribs.

Before I can comment Jack adds, "He hit the door frame getting in."

Tappen just shakes his head.

"What about Burly Man?" I say to all.

"Who?" Matt says, and gives Jack a stare.

"I tried that," Tappen mutters into his lap. "I'm the only one they want."

"A man has to work," I say, in the words of Manny.

Matt and Jack just stare at me.

"I'm going to turn myself in," Tappen says, keeping his eyes forward.

Go ahead and look at me, I want to say—*that's what the sunglasses are for.* "It looks like you done it already," I say.

From the front seat Jack says, "It was Gerald here's idea to come find you. We figured you were long gone—jumped a train or whatever you guys do."

"Sure, just like some hobo in a comic strip."

"I'm going to tell them everything I know," Tappen says.

"Which is what?" I say.

Tappen pauses. Jack nods for him to go on, like a lawyer does. Tappen says, "Oscar, he fell. At my job site. I decided to cover it up."

I wait for more, but nothing else gives. Tappen sobs. Jack reaches over the seat back, pats him on the knee.

"I never should've left him there at work that day," I say. "He wasn't in the best mood to begin with."

Tappen turns to me. We share a long glance, but I can't see through those dark glasses.

"Well, what now? You taking me in too?" I say to Matt and Jack.

"Why? You weren't there," Jack says.

"Or, were you?" Matt adds.

"No."

"So. Anything else you want to tell us?" Jack says.

I look them both in the eye, first Jack facing me, then Matt in the rear view mirror. "No. Thanks, but, no." I open the door, then pause. "Anyone spare any change?"

Matt and Jack shake their heads. "We fell for that one already."

"All right."

"Wait," Matt says. "Seriously? We do want to help."

"Then say it—say why you want to help. It's not 'cause I'm on the street. Look at all these people on the street. It's got to be in your records: I tried to kill myself. Three times. The first time I almost drowned. You'd think that woulda cured me."

This gets Tappen staring.

"Touché," Jack says. "Listen. Just say the word. The offer stands, if you know what I mean."

Meaning: *you tell us what you really found out.* "I think I'm good," I say. "Really. But, thanks."

I don't hop a train now. Why the hell should I? Not in a world where Eva Tappen did not run. She didn't confess either. She went ahead and let Tappen confess, knowing he would take the rap for her too and, unknowingly, for Oscar. Knowing a thing or two about a guy who's about to crack. Eva is hoping I'll go along. And I just might yet. Because I'm learning the truth I needed. Because Tappen must have developed his own version of the truth if he's so willing to own up. That and the fact that he is surely hoping for protection from the people he owes a whole ton of money, they who are about to yank a string and let him fall a long way down. Because, Matt and Jack must know that the whole truth is never cut and dried.

Still, I'm going to have to test out my theories if I ever am to move on.

Two days later, I try Niki's at 3:15. Matt and Jack aren't there but I ask a waitress if she's seen them. She says no but I could wait. So I take a booth. She pours me a coffee. I'm in the corner, facing the entrance of this Greek diner like the guy in the movie with all the exits covered.

It takes an hour, but they come and sit on either side of me, Matt to my right and Jack to my left. "Long time," Matt says.

"And good timing, too," Jack tells me. "We were just going to come find you. Turns out, we need to know what you know. Our head honchos want to know."

"You never been tortured," Matt says, "till you get summoned to my lieutenant's office and have to smell his patchouli."

Jack grimaces at that.

"Are you guys running me in?"

"What? No. You were our informant, for a day at least. So let's wrap this thing up."

I might never have been much of a better or gambler, but I got nothing to lose either. I hold up my hands, then let them flop on the booth vinyl. "What can I say? I tried Eva Tappen. She took me to her condo. She was sad, maybe a little distraught. Is that the word?"

"Distraught how?"

"She just wanted things resolved. She wasn't talking to her husband, apparently."

"But, she didn't tell you anything new? Nothing at all?"

"Me? No. She did offer to put me up at her place. Between you and me? I think she might have a kink for homeless guys . . ."

Jack nods along, smiling, eyes all wide.

"But I felt bad about it," I go on. "I'd come to spy and all. What? What is it?"

"Guess where we were this morning?" Matt says.

"Voodoo Doughnuts."

"Funny guy. No. We were talking to Eva Tappen."

In a flash I imagine cop cars pulling up, uniform officers blocking all exits. But it's just us and the regulars.

"Aka Eva Alvarez," Jack adds. "Oscar being her brother and all."

"She's still there?"

"She was, as of this morning."

If they were going to arrest me, I realize, they would have already done it by now. I feel a sensation new to me, warm in my belly and frisky in my brain, and it's not the coffee—I'm feeling cocky. I slap at the booth vinyl. Hell, I even grin. "Well, there you go. If there was anything fishy, she woulda flown the coop."

"Vamoosed," Matt says. "She still could."

"Can't say I'd blame her," I say. "I'm guessing having her hubby in jail doesn't really help the lifestyle. She'd do fine back home with what she's made of herself."

"Now there's a switch," Jack says. "Ole Mexico's a more promised land than we got right here."

"She's from Guatemala," I say. "People always make that mistake. Drove Oscar nuts."

Matt and Jack are sharing one of their glances across me, like they're the parents and I'm the black sheep kid in the middle.

I add, "Look, you guys, I'm sorry I didn't check in. It's just that, there was nothing new to learn. Nothing good anyway. You know how it is."

"Sure," Matt says.

"So, why come here?" Jack says to me.

"I guess I just wanted to say I'm sorry. Tie things up like you say. You did tell me to 'just say the word' after all."

Matt and Jack share that parental glance of theirs again.

"Here's the deal," I tell them, "I don't need Oscar. If anything, he probably needed me. It took all this crap to tell me that. What I really should do is thank you guys."

Matt raises his eyebrows. Jack nods.

"What is it now? Well, what is it?"

Jack pulls out an envelope, places it on the tabletop, and slides it over to me with fingertips. "Eva wanted you to have this. I guess Oscar did too, in his way. She was keeping it for Oscar. She gave it to us when we were there. She was very clear about it. After you left she was looking for you but couldn't find you, the way you, uh, move around."

"She said you would know how much it means," Matt says.

I stare at the envelope. If it's some kind of confession or goodbye letter, then I still might be screwed. "What happened at her place?" I say, stalling. "She didn't tell you nothing new?"

"Us? Nope. Just more wrapping things up. Checking Gerald Tappen's story against hers." For a moment longer than I think normal, Jack seems to eye me like poker players do looking for a tell. "You really have nothing else to add? Nothing at all?"

"I guess not," I say.

"Well, that's it then."

"It's a lot of money," Matt adds.

"Money?"

"Close to eight thousand dollars," Jack says before I can get a word out.

I snort, and shake my head, and force out a smile.

"Do you have a bank account?" Matt says.

"I do but it's not like there's anything in it." I've been saying that same sentence for so many years, I shake my head at that too. "So that's it? I just take the big check?"

"It's cash. Don't worry, the notes are legit. Verified by yours truly."

"We could go with you to the bank in case they don't believe you," Jack adds.

"That's okay. I don't want to put you guys out."

We sit there a moment. I sip my coffee. It's cold now, but inside me things are practically nice and toasty. I wonder if the money was Oscar's he was saving or a fund she was saving for him. I'm not going to fight it this time, and I'm not about to go ask her. Eva doesn't like questions.

"Wow, that Eva must really love Gerald Tappen," I say after a while.

"Yeah. And he her," Jack says.

I saw Amy once. I was on the bus, riding home after studying up at the Central Library like I'd been doing. It was the end of that following winter. Amy was standing at an intersection on NE Broadway, about as close to an I-5 onramp as you can get and still find a ride—and, I realized, not too far from my old hideaway. Her cardboard sign read: Recovering Addict, Need Ticket Home to Idaho, PLZ.

I had never gone to the hospital to see her or wherever they surely sent her to detox. It wouldn't have been good for her, or for me. We push each other's buttons, even though we were such a good team on the street. Sometimes you can't have one without the other.

She looked cleaned up, her hair combed. She had the puppy. It had grown into its long ears and thick paws. I smiled as my bus moved on, but I didn't wave. I don't know if she saw me. I swear I saw her little chin quivering as she stared straight ahead, hoping for the next car to spare a dollar.

I looked for her there every time my bus passed. I still tell myself that she was able to make her way back home and start over.

Gerald Tappen died in custody awaiting trial. Knifed in the gut. It was the old "mysterious circumstances." The paranoid in me wondered if Eva had her own brand of a Manny do the deed, her self-preservation kicking in over the guilt, but then I woke in the middle of the night with the horrid thought that it could easily have been the men he owed money to. Men like that had an army of far-worse Mannys—safeguarding forever what was already untouchable.

I can't believe it's been over a year, almost spring again. I have an apartment now. It's a one-room job in a low-income building and it will do just fine, thank you. Just having my own bathroom is like going on vacation for a guy like me. I even have a basic cell phone, pay as you go. The smart phone can wait.

I head out and down the front steps. It's morning. The clouds are high and sheer and it's almost sunny. I ride my new bicycle—old but new to me, a grown-up-sized cruiser. Two young guys with mustaches on fixed-gear bikes pass me. Type-A professionals in spandex zip by. Let them. I got no rush.

I coast past the four corners, eyeing the scene. The corners are empty except for a few wandering jonesers. The new posters in English and Spanish there read: *Better Work, A Better Life: Don't Let the Job Kill You*, with our location and hours listed in smaller print.

Our location is only a few blocks away. We got a small vacant lot with a fence to make day laborers feel safe and plenty more posters and notices and news.

Outside the fence there's already a long line of day laborers and the sometimes homeless—gringo and Latino, male and female. Some look hopeful, smiling and chatting. Some aren't looking too good.

I slip through the gate and lock up my bicycle outside our office, a salvaged mobile home. Once inside, I take another look from the window. The line runs down the block now. Some see me and nudge others to pay attention. So I head outside to get things rolling. Burly Manny follows me out with a clipboard—he's my assistant now. We pay him next to nothing, but he takes it. I open the gate, and I speak right up. "Everybody! Good morning. *Buenos días*. My name, is Travis . . ."

About the Author

Steve Anderson is the author of the Kaspar Brothers novels: *The Losing Role*, *Liberated*, and *Lost Kin*; *Under False Flags* is the prequel to his latest novel, *The Preserve*. Anderson was a Fulbright Fellow in Germany and is a literary translator of bestselling German fiction as well as a freelance editor. He lives in Portland, Oregon.

STEVE ANDERSON

FROM OPEN ROAD MEDIA

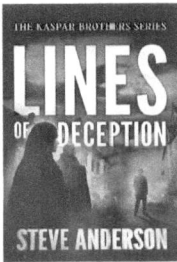

OPEN ROAD

INTEGRATED MEDIA

OPEN ROAD

INTEGRATED MEDIA

Find a full list of our authors and
titles at www.openroadmedia.com

FOLLOW US
@OpenRoadMedia